A GOBLIN POSTMAN CHILLER

RUNNING

ON

MOONLIGHT

PATRICIA BOW

This book was first published in 1998 by Cora Verlag GmbH under the title *Das Grab des Vampirs,* in German translation. *Running on Moonlight* is the original (and revised) English text.

Goblin Postman icon created by Patricia Bow

Cover images are used by permission of the owners, and in accordance with their Creative Commons licenses:
   Moonlit Drive photo by Suzanne Kirk
   (http://www.flickr.com/people/shezamm/)
   Runner photo by Alexandre Dulaunoy
   (http://www.flickr.com/people/adulau/)
   Dark Woods photo by Patti Haskins (http://pattihaskins.com)

Contents

Chapter 1

Breaking In

"WHAT I WANT TO KNOW," Jessie whispered, "is how come you didn't just go straight to the police?" She waved away a cloud of gnats. "What can we do? All by ourselves, I mean?"

"We can do plenty. We... " Pete lifted his head. A door banged somewhere nearby.

"Quick!" Jessie gave him a shove. "Hide!"

Pete dropped to the grass and crawled into the gap between a waist-high yew hedge and the yellow brick wall of the house. When Jessie tried to crawl in after him, he flapped a hand at her. "No room!"

Feet crunched on the cracked brick path around the corner of the house. Jessie started to panic. "What about me?"

"There!" Pete pointed.

She spun around and spotted a patch of tall flowers around a sun-dial. Enough cover for a cat, maybe! The footsteps crunched nearer. Jessie leaped, scrunched in among the stems and feathery leaves, and found an unexpected hollow under the disk of the sundial. Just enough of a hiding place, if she ducked her head and hugged her knees to her chest. And if her white sweater didn't show through the flowers, which were asters in all shades of pink and blue and purple.

She'd caught her breath and now she could see what was in front of her eyes. The sundial's stone pedestal was an eight-sided column three feet high. Something was carved on one side. Four shapes, plain to see in the broken green-gold light. A circle at the top, a half-circle

1

below that, then a crescent. At the bottom was another circle with the space inside coloured black.

She gazed at the carvings, barely aware of being puzzled. Nine-tenths of her attention was on the path beside the house, where a man in dark grey work pants and shirt was walking past toward the front. A scissoring of legs, a clink of steel as he tossed a bunch of keys in his hand.

The jingling faded. Jessie held her breath. No sound now.

Pete's head poked out of the gap behind the yew hedge, dark hair raked over his eyes. He looked left and right. Then he scrambled up and dashed along the side of the house and around the corner to the back. Jessie crawled from among the asters and ran to catch up.

"It was back here! I was with my dad, delivering kibble." Pete had an after-school job in his family's Pet Emporium. He earned next to nothing, but he would have done it for free. For the animals.

They were moving right under a row of windows. Reckless, crazy, dangerous! Trust Pete to jump into trouble with both feet. Jessie looked up as she scurried, expecting to see faces frowning behind glass, windows flying up, shouts of *trespasser*! But nobody showed. Yet.

The house was big, square, and built of pale-yellow brick, with large white-framed windows and elegantly carved white wooden trim under the eaves. It was a hundred years old, so Jessie had been told. The third storey was smaller than the other two, with walls all glass, and it looked like the top tier on a wedding cake.

It actually was a beautiful house, when you got a close look at it. There was nothing sinister about it. Not even when it stood black against a bloody sunset sky the way it did now, with the red light flooding through that top storey.

Maybe it was just that it sat so quiet and smug behind its stone fence and iron gate, its trees and acres of lawn, its flower beds shaped in circles and crescents. The property was big enough for a park, but nobody ever cut through here, not even the older, wilder kids. The house kept itself to itself, the way Dr. Erasmus did. It didn't mix with the neighbourhood.

Jessie thought of her father, and that last bit of work done here, at the Erasmus house, before his death. She often thought of her dad. Gone, taken away from her, and in that terrible way. Maybe that was why a glimpse of this house always put her under a cloud.

"It was here." Pete knelt at a small window in the stone foundation.

Jessie squeezed in beside him. "I can't see a thing!"

A grille of steel bars was bolted to the window frame. A shade covered the inside of the glass. A sliver of gap showed along each side of the shade, not wide enough to let Jessie properly see anything beyond.

"My dad was inside, getting paid." Pete nodded at the back door to their right. It stood a few inches open. "I was out here, bored, so I looked in the windows. The shades were up then."

"Uh-huh." Jessie wasn't being sceptical. She'd have done the same. Anybody would, given a chance to see what Dr. Erasmus was up to.

"I was going to tell my dad to come look, but somebody came and pulled the shade down inside. I knew there was no use after that."

"He's some kind of scientist, Dr. Erasmus, right?"

"That doesn't give him the right to torture helpless animals!"

"I know, I know. I still don't know why you dragged me here."

"As a witness, of course!" Pete skewered her with his eyes. They were usually dark and soft, or bright and laughing, but he could make them steel-hard when he wanted. Like now. "You know what'll happen if I tell the Humane Society. They'll phone Dr. Erasmus and he'll say, 'Sure, no problem, come and look.'" Pete waved his hands generously. "Then, when they come, the animals will be gone. Or there'll be different animals, and they'll all be okay. And he'll say the other ones were never there. And who'll believe me then?"

"I'd believe you. Your parents would too."

"That wouldn't be enough."

Jessie squinted into the gap next to the shade. The lights were on in there, but all she could see was a sliver of grey floor. "Well, we can't be witnesses if we can't see anything."

"Right. We'll have to go in." Pete got up and took a step toward the back door.

"Go in! No way! It'll be trespassing! We'll get caught!"

"But if I can prove... "

"Sh!" She caught his arm.

A jingling sound came from around the corner of the house. From the front.

They stared at each other for one long breathless second. Then Pete was off and running. Not away, of course not. Straight for the open back door. "Pete! No!" Jessie breathed, but he was already inside the house.

Chapter 2

Locked In

IT WOULDN'T BE the first time Pete had pitched himself into a great big mess, always for the best of reasons. Usually something to do with animals. And it wouldn't be the first time Jessie had fallen in after him, spluttering protests.

She darted in through the door. "I must be out of my mind!"

They stood on a landing with stairs leading up to the right and down in front. Down they went, skidding and grabbing at the hand rail, to the cellar. At the bottom of the stairs was a dim storage room stocked with sacks of hamster kibble and puppy chow and boxes of lizard food: canned mealworms

Pete went straight to the door on the left side of the room and opened it softly. On the landing above, a door closed and a lock went *snick*. Then the stairs creaked. Somebody was coming down after them.

No time to look at each other, no time to breathe. They slipped into the next room as if their feet were buttered. Jessie eased the door closed. It had a frosted window that you couldn't see anything through, except light.

"Suppose he comes in here?" she whispered.

"Hide. Lots of places."

It was a huge room. It ran the length of the house, Jessie guessed. Bare 100-watt bulbs in the ceiling flooded every corner with a harsh white light. Cages stood everywhere. On wide shelves along the walls, stacked two and three deep on a row of tables up the centre of the room. Stacked under the tables, too. Everywhere you looked, steel wires glistened in the glare.

Shiny white walls. Bare concrete floor inset with covered drains. It looked like a science lab at school. It smelled like a pet store. Not bad, just strong.

It sounded like a pet store, too. Small drab birds hopped and chirped. Pete frowned in at them. "Sparrows? Why would he want those?" A dog yipped at one end of the room, another dog ruff-ruffed back at it. There was a riot of squeaking and chittering, wood shavings crunching, teeth picking at wires, *ping!*

"What's this thing?" Jessie bent over a cage made of fine wire mesh. She came nose-to-nose with a lizard the length of her thumb, tail included. Its skin was plastic-shiny, black flashing to purple and green as it moved. She nosed nearer to get a better look and it snapped tiny jaws at her.

"Look!" Pete called softly. He was squatting in front of a big cage. "Here's the cat I saw. Look at its paws!"

Jessie knelt beside Pete. The cat's feet were bandaged. The forelegs, in their white wrappings, looked wrong: too short. Jessie tried to think the best. "It must've been in an accident, and Dr. Erasmus found it, and... "

"It's not the only one. There's a dog over there, with part of a hind leg missing."

"So he rescues wounded animals. That's good, right?"

"Yeah, right. The great Dr. Erasmus."

"I don't see why you're so suspicious!"

"Shh!"

In the storage room next door, feet scuffed the concrete floor. The doorknob rattled. Jessie ducked in between two cages under a table. No cover at all, if the man decided to bend down and look. But the best she could do. Pete dashed and flattened himself against the

6

end wall behind a stack of cardboard boxes.

Jessie held dead still and breathed shallowly. The doorknob rattled again. The pattering and cheeping and barking suddenly stopped, as if all the animals were hunkering down, trying not to be noticed.

Hard shoe leather tapped the floor. Jessie watched a pair of dark grey pant legs, with dusty black oxfords on the bottom, as they paced back and forth, in no hurry.

She was so intent on the shoes that she hardly heard a rustling at floor level. Then something touched her arm and she looked down.

The mesh of the cage beside her arm was covered with little green-purple-black knife-shapes. Tiny lizards, a dozen, twenty. Pale things darted from their jaws. Their tongues, Jessie saw, fascinated.

All the miniscule tongues were flicking at her arm, trying to reach her through the mesh. *Like they're tasting me. Like I'd be their one meal for the week and they can't wait to eat.*

The thought made her flinch. Her other arm bumped the table leg. Cages rattled.

The shoes stood still. Jessie held her breath. Then the shoes moved again. Metal scraped across wood. The shoes walked away. A switch snapped and the lights went out, leaving them in the dark. The door closed. There was a solid-sounding *click*.

Jessie waited a minute, just to be sure, then crawled out. "Well, thank you, Peter Oliveiri!" she hissed. "Thank you very much! We're locked in! And I can't see! And things've been trying to eat me!"

"Don't panic, none of these guys are dangerous."

"Those lizards think they are!"

Pete was moving toward the exit, she could tell by the sound. She wished he'd be quieter. A pale square showed in that direction: the frosted glass of the door. Feeling her way along the edge of the table, she tiptoed to the door beside him and listened. No sound on the other side. She tried the handle, but it was locked, sure enough.

"So what now, Mr. Super Sleuth?"

"Can't you do something?"

"Me!"

"Your dad was a locksmith, right?"

"He never taught me to pick locks!"

"Okay, then." Pete raised a fist.

Jessie caught his arm. "Idiot! You'll cut yourself! Besides, somebody'll hear."

"What other way is there? We'll never get out a window, not with those bars."

The darkness seemed less solid now: their eyes were adjusting. Pete detoured around the end of the row of tables, reached and pulled at one of the shades. It flew up with a whirr and a bang. They froze. When nothing else happened, and nobody burst through the door, he raised the other shades: quietly.

The light that came through the barred windows was blue, just enough to see by. Behind the glinting wires of the cages the animals were moving again. Eyes gleamed, tails switched. Scuttling sounds came from near the floor. Jessie kept expecting something to crawl up her leg. She edged away from the cages.

"This place creeps me out."

"Look, the cat's gone." Pete touched an empty space on the table. "He took it away. What for?"

"Never mind that! How do we get out? Is there another door?"

"Let's look."

They walked in single file, Jessie first, between the rustling cages. And yes, there was another door. It was in the wall farthest from the end where they'd come in, a solid wooden door with no glass. It wasn't locked and it opened soundlessly. They filed through.

There was no window here. Just enough blue light came through the door to show a small room about three metres square. It was a

8

dead end.

But it wasn't empty. Down the middle, from floor to ceiling, glimmering metal striped the air. More metal rods ran across the ceiling and down the back and side walls.

"Will you look at that!" Pete shook his head in wonder.

Half the room was a giant cage.

Jessie stepped close to the bars and ran her fingertips down them. They didn't look like steel. This was a whiter, warmer metal, with a softer gleam. She knew a little about metals, from watching and talking with her dad. "Silver?" she asked wonderingly.

Pete laughed. "You're nuts. That much silver would cost a fortune!"

Jessie touched the lock, a square box on the bars in front of her. "Pete. I think … maybe … I think this was Dad's last job."

Pete pressed his face against the bars. "Jessie! Something's in there. Something big."

She wouldn't have seen it if he hadn't told her. She could barely make it out now. It was just a dark shape huddled in the exact centre of the cage floor, with two pale streaks across its body.

"I'll bet it's a bear, or an ape, or something else ol' Erasmus could really get into torturing." Pete grabbed the lock and shook it.

"You're not letting it out!" Jessie backed off. "We're in enough trouble already." But whatever the creature was, she couldn't take her eyes off it.

Then the two pale streaks moved and became hands, and a pale blob lifted from the dark mass and became a face. The shape unfolded upward and drifted toward them.

Pete jumped back. Jessie's heart thumped.

The shape stopped short of the bars and gazed at them.

Not a bear, not an ape. A boy.

"Help me!" he whispered.

Chapter 3

The Caged Boy

PETE WAS SPEECHLESS. All he could do was stare.

"How'd you get in there?" Jessie demanded. "Who put you in there?"

"I can't explain, there's no time. They could be coming down here any minute!"

The boy stretched his hands toward her, but his fingertips stopped short of the bars. She reached through and his hand wrapped around hers. His fingers were strong, bony and cold. His grip hurt her fingers.

In the dark, she could only see that he was very pale. Pale hair spilled over his shoulders. White skin. He looked like something that lived in the dark, *like one of those white spiders in our basement*, the thought jumped into her head. Pale eyes, the brightest thing about him. His clothes were dark, some sort of sweater and jeans.

"It's okay!" she whispered. "We'll get you out! Pete, this is awful!"

"I know." Pete shook the lock again. "Solid."

"The key: it's on the wall by the door," the boy breathed.

Jessie tried to free her hand, but he held on desperately tight. Pete darted away and was back in two seconds. He slid the key into the lock, twisted, and threw the door open, inward.

The boy let go of Jessie's hand and leaped back as the door swung near him. Then he whipped through the opening and out into the main room.

Jessie and Pete crowded after him. It was darker now. A storm of barking and miowling and rattling and cheeping burst from the gloom as they clattered through.

"That's locked too," Pete said as the boy gripped the knob of the door with the glass panel. The boy looked around, grabbed one of the cages and rammed it at the window. The glass shattered.

"Are you nuts?" Pete snatched the cage out of the boy's hands.

"I'm sorry. I think it's hurt. Some of the glass got in the cage." The boy raised his hands to his mouth, and Jessie saw dark, shiny stripes on the white skin.

"You're cut!"

"Never mind! Hurry! They're coming!"

And now that Jessie had found the caged boy, *they* suddenly loomed huge in her imagination. *They* weren't just the people of the house, people who'd naturally be miffed to find strange kids sneaking around in their basement, people who'd yell a bit and chivvy them out the door. *They* were people who kept kids caged like animals.

She reached through the shattered window, bent her arm to avoid the jagged pieces still stuck in the frame, groped for the thumb latch and twisted it. As she pulled her hand back, pain streaked across her palm. Warm blood trickled down her fingers. The pale boy gasped.

"It's nothing!" No time to worry about it. She threw the door open and it crashed against the wall. The boy dashed through.

Pete climbed to his feet with maddening slowness. He was cradling something in his hands. Jessie grabbed him by an elbow and rushed him through the storage room and up the stairs to the back door.

"Careful!" he yelped. "Careful! I'll drop it!"

A door slammed upstairs. Feet thudded. The strange boy fumbled with the latch on the back door for three long heart-thumping seconds, while the feet pounded nearer.

And then they were out and flying. Skid at the sharp right turn on the brick path, a dead run alongside the house, then across the lawn and onto the broad driveway. Then it was a race for the gate, a tall grille that made a barred silhouette across the lit pavement beyond. Jessie ran as if her feet were on springs.

Beside her the pale boy ran with his face lifted to the sky, hair streaming. He looked like a hawk set free, like he was so bursting with joy that any moment now he could take off and fly. He caught her eye and flashed her a wild grin, and she flung a laugh back at him.

They hit the closed gate together and bounced off. It rang like an iron bell. Pete came panting up behind them, still cupping his hands as if he was carrying water.

"Locked," Jessie gasped. "Should've known!"

They remembered the man with his jingling handful.

"We can't get over that." Pete looked up at the nine-foot stretch of vertical bars. There were no handy crosspieces, no iron curlicues, nothing to get a foot on.

They clustered next to the gate, looking out through the bars. A street lamp stood a few metres up the road. Across the street a row of trees and lilac bushes stirred in the breeze. Not a flicker of light showed from the houses beyond.

"It's like we're miles away from anyone else." Jessie shivered. With the sun gone, there wasn't much warmth left in the September air.

The boy straightened his thin shoulders. "I'm sure we can help each other over the wall."

She wondered where he came from. The way he talked was different, strangely adult. His voice was low and smooth, the words clear-cut as new dimes.

Pete was staring at the lump of fur in his cupped hands.

12

"What is that thing?" Jessie leaned in for a look.

"It's a gerbil. It's dead. It bled to death." He stabbed a look at the other boy, then turned his back on them and walked along to where the stone wall started. A row of Lombardy poplars stood close against it on the inside like a second, taller fence. He knelt, scooped a hollow in the drift of dry leaves between the trees and the wall, set the gerbil's body down and gently covered it. Then stood up again, wiping his hands on his pants.

"Guess they're not going to bother chasing us," Jessie said. Then she caught her breath. A cry rose near the house. Then another.

If it was a cry. It sounded more like the top note on a violin, or a far-off train whistle. But it meant something to the strange boy. "Over the wall! Quick!"

"But what is that?" Jessie stared back along the driveway.

"Hounds. Come on!"

"Hounds?" Pete echoed. "That's no kind of a dog!"

The boy was already out of sight between the poplars and the wall. Jessie pushed in after him. Pete was right on her heels.

"Here!" In front of her a dark shape flowed up the wall. Jessie felt for something to dig fingertips into, any crevice or roughness, but the stones were smooth.

"Grab on!" A white hand thrust down at her. She grabbed it with her right and felt a burn as the clotted cut on her palm broke open. She barely noticed the pain, being at that moment hauled up into the air like a sack of road salt.

She grabbed with her left hand and scrabbled with her knees and then she was straddling the wall facing the boy. Their hands were still locked together.

He let go suddenly. "I've bled all over you."

"Doesn't matter. Hurry up, Pete!"

Something shrilled near the gate.

Pete leaped for the top of the wall and fell back as his fingers slipped. Jessie's heart crowded into her throat.

"Here!" the other boy held down a hand.

"I'm okay!" Pete jumped again, got fingertips over the top and then an elbow. Jessie hauled at his jacket.

The poplars swayed as something shouldered through them.

"Go!" yelled the boy.

Pete hooked a foot over the top of the wall, yanked himself up and kept on rolling.

The others leaped. They sprawled on the grass on the other side. Pushed and pulled each other to their feet. And ran.

Chapter 4

Lucan

THE BASEBALL DIAMOND seemed like a safe place to stop. It was five blocks from the Erasmus house, and whatever hound had tracked them to the wall must have stayed there. It hadn't come after them on the street.

The bleachers were almost full. Out on the brilliantly floodlit field the Finnismore Flyers were pounding the Wilston Wranglers, and all their parents and brothers and sisters and friends were there. They were making a lot of noise.

Many of them were people Jessie knew, kids from her Grade 10 class at school. She hoped nobody would spot them and come over. She wasn't up to answering questions right now, even if she could have thought of any answers.

But all eyes were on the game. Nobody spared a glance for the three kids who stood behind the bleachers at the side of the concession booth, bent over gasping.

In fact, only two were bent over gasping. Jessie and Pete were winded, but the strange boy wasn't even breathing fast. He stood there calmly gazing around. And nobody had noticed them, as far as Jessie could tell, except for one man sitting by himself in the top row of the bleachers. He glanced over his shoulder at them, then looked away, not interested.

"What have we done?" Jessie slumped against the Fiberglas wall of the booth and thumped her forehead with her fists. "How many laws did we break?"

"Trespassing." Pete ticked them off on his fingers. "Damage to property. Maybe kidnapping. How's your cut?"

She looked at her palm. Under the smears of blood the cut was closed again. "Looks okay." She flexed her hand. The cut pulled, but it didn't hurt much. She looked at the strange boy. "You got cut too."

"It's nothing. Hardly a nick." He spread his right hand to show the fingers striped with dried blood. The cut wasn't visible. "You saved my life," he said softly. In the patch of shadow behind the bleachers, you could only see that his eyes were very pale. Jessie guessed they'd be sky-blue in daylight. His hair floated in the slightest breeze, like spider silk.

Pete, shorter and darker and solider, turned to face him. "Saved your life? We let you out of that stupid cage, but that's all."

"My father was going to kill me."

They were silent. You saw things like this in movies, you even read about them in the news, kids getting killed by their parents. But you never believed they could really be true, Jessie thought. Not in the world she knew.

"You mean, that man with the keys," she began.

"Him! No, he's just one of the help. My father is Dr. August Erasmus. I am Lucan Erasmus." He sounded quietly proud.

"Didn't know Erasmus had a son." Pete's sceptical streak was showing a mile wide.

"I was raised by my mother's people, after she died. A long way from here. My father wasn't interested. Until lately."

"But why would he want to kill you?" Jessie protested. "You're kidding, right? I mean, his own son!"

"You don't believe me." Lucan's eyes flicked from Jessie to Pete. "Are you going to turn me in?"

Pete's eyebrows went up. "Who to?"

"The police. Or my father."

16

"I wouldn't send a dog back to that guy. Especially not a dog. What's he after with those animals?"

"Something to do with his experiments. Just a guess. He doesn't tell me things."

Jessie uncurled from the wall. "I'm dry as a bone after all that running!" She led the way along the side of the booth to the front, where yellow light fanned out across the grass.

As she rounded the corner, the boy behind the counter jumped back and crashed into the pop cooler, nearly tipping it over. It was obvious he'd been leaning out, listening. He'd heard what they'd been saying. His eyes goggled at her, fascinated.

"He'll tell!" Lucan hissed in her ear.

"Don't be silly." Jessie had seen the boy at school. He looked like a football fullback: two hundred pounds of muscle packed inside a too-small Finnismore Parks Department T-shirt. A pin-on name tag said KENNY.

And now she saw that he wasn't staring at her. He was staring at Lucan, not blinking. You'd think his eyes were tied there with strings.

"Kenny!" Jessie tapped a toonie on the counter. He blinked rapidly, then looked at her as if he'd only just realized she was there. "Can of cola, please."

Kenny smiled feebly and sold them drinks. He'd be no harm, Jessie thought.

Cans of pop in hand, they walked to the street. They stopped on the sidewalk with their backs to the traffic. Out here, anybody could see them, but nobody could listen.

"Okay," Jessie looked Lucan up and down. "Where can you go? Got any other relatives around here?"

"No."

"What about the Children's Aid?" Pete said.

"No!" Lucan backed away. "No police, no Children's Aid. They'll just hand me straight back to him."

"But we'd tell how we found you." Jessie said. "We'd show them that cage."

"Won't matter. They'll believe him, not you."

"But... "

"All right, if you're not going to help me!" He spun and started away along the sidewalk.

Jessie ran after him and grabbed his hand. It seemed wrong, a shame and a waste, to just let him go, after all the panic and effort of the rescue. "Of course we're going to help you!"

Pete trotted over. "He might be too old for Children's Aid, anyway. Lucan? How old are you?"

"I turn sixteen on Friday."

Jessie looked at him in surprise. Sixteen! But now she could get a good look at him, she could see it. He looked a lot older than Pete, who was fourteen, same age as she was. Pete was still the same solid, big-boned kid she'd known since grade four, just a couple of sizes larger than he'd been back then.

"So, no problem," she said. "All you have to do is stay out of sight 'til Friday. That's just three days from now. After you turn sixteen, nobody can make you do anything you don't want to. Right, Pete?"

"'S right."

"You can go live with your mother's family. Your grandparents?"

He smiled at her. A strange smile, more in the warming eyes than in the closed, curved mouth. "Yes. But until then I have nowhere. And my father... " His mouth flattened. "He's good at getting what he wants."

"Why should he know where you are? We'll hide you."

18

There, it was out. Right away she started to worry. But she knew there'd be no taking it back.

The boy's eyes lit strangely. "Do you mean it?"

"I said it, didn't I?" She was getting more worried by the second.

"Wouldn't that be against the law? Hiding a runaway?"

"Maybe, I don't know. Locking a kid in a cage and telling him he's going to be killed, that's got to be against the law!"

"Darn right," Pete said. "I vote you hide him."

"Me?"

"You know what my house is like."

Pete and his family lived above their store, Oliveiri's Pet Emporium, on King Street. He had two older brothers, two younger sisters, two parents, a grandmother, and three cats. Trying to hide an extra person there would be like leading an elephant through downtown Finnismore and hoping nobody would notice.

"Okay, it's got to be my house, then." Jessie looked at Lucan. "You'd have to stay in the attic, and it'll be boring and it won't be very comfy. And you'd have to be very, very quiet."

"You're really going to help me," he said flatly, as if he only now believed it. "You're going to protect me."

She took a breath. "Yes."

"You won't give me away? You won't tell?"

"Of course I won't, I promise."

He was staring. "This is true? Really true?"

"Lucan! I promised!"

"Jessie doesn't break promises," Pete said. "She's fierce that way."

Lucan's eyes were shining. "I won't forget this. Ever."

A roar broke from the bleachers. Someone had hit a homer, and the runners were racing around the bases. A good time to leave, Jessie decided.

19

As they started along the street she glanced back once, to see if anybody was watching them go. Only one head turned. It belonged to the man sitting by himself in the top row.

"Did you see that man in the back looking at us?" she asked Pete. "Do you know him?"

He glanced back. "I don't notice anybody, specially. What does he look like?"

"Well, he... " She frowned. "I don't know."

She tried to put the man out of her mind, but it was strange. The face, so unnoticeable, was strangely hooked into her mind. It was linked to some buried memory. And all she knew was, the memory was bad.

Chapter 5

Marianne

JESSIE LED LUCAN into the house by the back way, along the lane behind the houses. It was dark here, away from the streetlights. If a neighbour happened to look out a window, they wouldn't see much. She guided him in through the gate in the fence, through the back yard, and past the compost bin. She was glad he couldn't see the un-mown grass and the weedy borders along the fence and compare them to his father's gorgeous gardens.

The back door was locked, but Jessie had her own set of keys. It was eight-thirty. Aunt Stephanie worked in the city, half an hour's drive away. She wasn't due home until nine. And Marianne made a point of staying out with her friends until the very last minute before curfew, which was nine o'clock on a school night, as often as possible. So it should have been easy.

Lucan looked around curiously, blinking against the sudden light, as she hustled him through the kitchen and along the hall to the front and up the stairs.

"Guess it all looks pretty cruddy to you," she muttered. Dr. Erasmus's son had to be used to posh living, no matter where he grew up.

Aunt Stephanie's house was 80 years old. It wasn't beautiful or dignified, like some old houses: like the Erasmus house, for example. It was just old, with something always needing to be fixed: the roof or the furnace or the plumbing.

A narrow, plain house, just like Aunt Steffie. And just like me,

Jessie thought, as her thin reflection flicked across the mirror at the top of the stairs, followed by Lucan's tall slice of darkness.

"I'll bring you something to eat as soon as I can. Here's the bathroom." She opened a door beside the mirror and flipped the light switch.

Lucan looked in and nodded politely.

"You should use it now." Thoughts of midnight disasters trampled through her mind. "Or else you might have to wait 'til tomorrow morning, when everybody's gone out again. That's a long time to wait if you have to, you know, go."

"Oh, right," Lucan said. "Okay."

The door closed behind him. Jessie sagged against the mirror and let out a long, shaky breath. She saw trouble crowding in on every side.

Suppose Lucan just *had* to use the bathroom in the middle of the night? Or suppose he turned on the attic light, and Aunt Steffie saw its glow on the leaves of the silver maple outside her window? Or suppose he forgot to be careful, and walked around? The attic floor was so creaky you could hear a mouse scamper, and Steffie was a light sleeper. Or suppose...

She snapped upright. A door along the hall opened and Marianne stepped out. She stopped, slashed a look at Jessie, then closed her door with a snap. She had on her white satin dressing gown and cradled an armload of plastic bottles and tubes. (Marianne had ostentatiously moved her hair-care supplies into the security of her room the day Jessie had come to live with them, a year ago.) She kept her eyes glued on Jessie as she minced along the hall in her fur-trimmed, court-heeled satin slippers.

Oh no! Why'd she have to stay home tonight of all nights?

Marianne reached for the bathroom door. It didn't open.

"Somebody in there?"

22

"No, it, um, it's locked. It locked behind me, accidentally, when I came out."

"Huh. Never knew that to happen before." She wrenched at the knob again. Then straightened up, tossed back her long, curly red mane, and skewered Jessie with another look. Marianne liked to make the most of her one extra year and two extra inches of height.

Jessie shrugged and looked helpless.

"So you're just going to stand there like a dummy?"

"Um, I don't know how to get it open."

"Screwdriver. Basement."

"I wouldn't know where to look."

Marianne rolled her eyes to heaven. Then set down her armload of bottles on the floor beside the bathroom door and pointed at them. "Don't touch those!" She click-clacked down the stairs.

As soon as Jessie judged that Marianne had reached the kitchen she thumped softly on the door. "Come out!" she whispered. "Hurry!"

The door opened and Lucan stuck his head out. "Who was that?"

"My cousin. Major pain. Come on!" She grabbed his arm and pulled him along the hall to the back, where a door opened into what looked like an empty closet. A leather strap dangled from the ceiling.

Jessie grabbed the strap and swung her weight on it, and the ceiling opened. A steel staircase unfolded downward, grating and squealing like a pen full of pigs. The bottom step thumped on the floor at their feet.

Lucan laughed. "That's amazing!"

"Go! Go!" She pushed him at the stairs and he whisked up and out of sight. Then she grabbed the bottom step and hoisted the contraption back into the ceiling. It complained so loud, you'd think the neighbours would hear. Marianne sure would.

Jessie was back beside the mirror, as if she'd never moved, when

Marianne came up the front stairs holding a screwdriver in her fist like a dagger.

She didn't even glance at the door leading to the attic, so maybe it hadn't been as loud as all that. She flicked her eyes at the open bathroom door, then at Jessie.

Jessie lifted a shoulder. "Guess what, I got it open. It must've been just stuck."

"Well, isn't that a funny thing." Marianne's eyes drilled into Jessie's as if she was digging for a criminal confession.

Born suspicious, that one. Jessie turned her back and went into her own room, the one closest to the attic stairs. The ceiling creaked above her head. *Oh, Lucan.* You'd think he'd know enough to keep still!

A FEW MINUTES LATER Aunt Stephanie came home. Jessie heard the front door close and ran down the stairs. Aunt Steffie had dropped her briefcase by the front door and was kicking off her black high-heeled shoes. "Now for a good long soak." She set a foot on the bottom step, then stopped and sniffed. The air was heavy with the scent of Mango Bliss bath oil. She closed her eyes and groaned softly.

"Yup, she beat you to it," Jessie said. "Are you hungry? I'll heat up some soup."

"You're an angel. I've had *such* a day!" She limped into the living room and collapsed on the sofa.

Jessie raced to the kitchen, opened a can of chicken noodle soup and started it simmering on the stove. Then she snatched a plastic grocery bag from a drawer and piled food into it. A banana, some granola bars, foil-wrapped cheese, a pumpernickel roll, two cans of ginger ale.

She thought of the squealing attic stairs, added a can of machine oil from under the sink and stuck a roll of paper towels under her

24

arm.

When she looked into the living room, the TV was on. Aunt Steffie's eyes were closed, head tilted back, mouth open. She was snoring gently. Jessie sneaked past. Steffie wouldn't hear a thing, she thought guiltily.

Up the stairs, quick. The water was still running in the bathroom. The attic stairs squealed again when she pulled them down. Each step yelped at her weight.

At least he'd had the sense to keep the light off. At the top of the stairs she stopped to search the dark with her eyes. She'd never much liked the attic: a dusty, dreary cavern stuffed with boxes of books nobody would ever want to read again, broken chairs and lamps, cartons of unidentified electronic parts, and stacks of *Canadian Geographic* that smelled of mildew.

"Over here!"

Jessie jumped. Until that moment she hadn't caught a hint of where he was. Even now she could barely make him out. He had found an old folding cot, and unfolded it. He crouched on the bare, thin mattress with knees folded up and arms wrapped around them, the same way he'd been sitting when they'd found him in the cage.

For a moment she felt confused and lost and lonely. The feeling flooded over her so suddenly and strongly that she was sure, somehow, it came from him.

"Here's some food." She set the bag on the cot beside him. "Wait, I'll be right back!"

Quick down the staircase, into her room, rip the wool blanket from under the quilted coverlet and up again, breathless. She tossed the blanket at him and he caught and swirled it like a bullfighter's cloak. His smile made a brief white flash in the gloom.

"Try not to walk around, it makes noise," she said. "Okay?"

"Okay."

25

"Better keep the light off, too. Sorry. But you don't want to be caught, do you?"

"I don't mind the dark." He smiled again, closed-mouth, and it seemed to her that his eyes grew brighter. "How is your hand?"

She opened and closed it. "It's fine. It was just a scratch. Got to go now." She started down, but his voice stopped her.

"Do you realize that some of my blood probably got into your cut? That time I pulled you up on the wall."

"Well, that shouldn't be... " An ugly thought poked its head up. A reason why he might be so pale and thin. "You don't mean you... you're... "

He laughed, a quick breath. "No, I don't have some dreadful fatal disease."

She laughed too, relieved and ashamed.

"I'm just thinking," he said, "it means we have a special bond, now that we've shared blood. Like in those old western movies. We're blood brothers." His mouth bent up. "Blood siblings?"

"Well, it's funny," she said awkwardly, "but for a moment there I thought I was feeling your feelings."

"It was the blood, Jessie. It's bonded us. Blood is the strongest thing there is." He wasn't laughing now, not even smiling. He meant it.

"Yes, well, I better oil those stairs."

She scrambled down. Dr. Erasmus was known as "different." Maybe he wasn't the only one in the family who was a bit strange.

The can of oil and the paper towels sat at the bottom of the steel staircase. Jessie slathered oil on all the moving parts, anointing every joint, hinge and bolt. Then she heaved it up into the ceiling. It slithered up, complaining quietly. More oil, more ups and downs, and it moved with barely a whisper.

There: one less worry. Jessie closed the door and went downstairs

26

to trash the oil-soaked paper towels, wash her hands and pull the boiling soup off the stove.

IT WAS DARK and getting darker. There wasn't enough air to breathe. Someone was walking around her, blocking up the doors and windows, shutting her in. Shutting her into the dark.

One window was left: a square with rounded corners. She crawled toward it. Then half of it blacked out as a face looked in. It smiled at her and she felt herself dying.

Chapter 6

Vanished

SHE WOKE sitting bolt upright, gasping for air. Bad dream. Which was nothing new: she'd had it before, that same dream, a dozen times in the past year. Why did that face keep haunting her?

The ceiling quivered above her head. The dream faded. Something was walking around up there. No, not walking. Jumping! Leaping with muffled thuds across the floor above her ceiling and on toward the front of the house, where Steffie's room was.

Lucan, no!

Jessie flung back her quilt and dashed to the door. Marianne was already out in the hall in her white satin pyjamas. Steffie's door opened and she came out tying the sash of her red chenille robe.

"What the heck is up there?" Marianne looked slyly at Jessie.

She yawned. "Big ol' raccoon, probably."

"Oh, no!" Steffie looked up at the ceiling. "I'll have to call in someone to trap it."

Marianne waved both hands. "Not to worry, Mom, there's no trick to getting rid of raccoons." She started toward the closet at the end of the hall. "This kid at school showed me. His dad's a pest control guy."

"No!" Jessie squeaked.

"Oh, why not?" Marianne smiled unpleasantly.

"If it's a raccoon, it, uh, it could have rabies!"

"Jessie's right, Marianne. And they can be fierce when they're cornered. Better not mess with it."

"Well, somebody has to. If Dad were here he'd take a look. He's not, so I guess it has to be me." Marianne didn't even glance at her mother as she said this, but Jessie did. Steffie's face tightened up all over.

Marianne was inside the closet now, pulling the stairs down. She stopped and sniffed the air. *Machine oil.* She slipped Jessie another smirk.

She knows.

Marianne started up. Jessie came right behind her. "Girls! Be careful!" Steffie called from below. "Don't go near it!"

As soon as Jessie had her head above the top of the stairs, she looked for the cot. It was almost invisible in its dark corner. Maybe Marianne would miss it.

Or not. Marianne crossed the floor and reached for the chain hanging from the rafters. *Click*, and a muddy yellow light showed the attic in all its dusty squalor. Nobody was on the cot or near it.

Good for you, Lucan!

Jessie climbed all the way out onto the floor. Cold air whiffled past her ankles.

"So where's our raccoon?" Marianne picked her way daintily between the stacks of cardboard boxes and herds of three-legged chairs to the front of the attic. A window in the gable, about a foot square, was open halfway. The shutters outside swung in the wind. There was no screen.

"Got in here and out again," Jessie said. "I guess it climbed up that tree out there."

"And opened the shutters all by itself?"

"Could've. They have clever hands."

"Mm, I guess. Who left this window up?" Marianne sliced a look at Jessie. "Careless!"

"I didn't," she began hotly, then saw the trap. If not her, then

29

who? Could raccoons open sash windows? She put on a clueless face. "Oh, well. I forgot, I guess."

Marianne reached through the window to close the shutters, then pushed down the sash. She strolled around the attic, poking behind a scarred old wardrobe here, under a broken table there, careful to keep her lovely pyjamas unsmudged. At the cot she stopped and nudged something out from beneath with a slippered foot. The plastic bag.

"Forgot that too?"

"Yeah." Jessie picked it up. She could tell by the weight that nothing was gone from it. Lucan hadn't eaten a thing.

Marianne scanned the attic, hands on hips. "I'd've sworn you were hiding somebody up here. A boy."

"A boy! Like I would!"

"Yeah, I should've known better, right? What boy would want to hide away with you?" She looked around one last time. "Even Pete Oliveiri. You don't have fur and a tail, so why would he be interested?"

BACK IN HER ROOM, Jessie took care not to look in the mirror on her dressing table. She put out the light and got back into bed.

That was just Marianne being her usual poisonous self. *It's not true. Boys do like me. I just don't make a big fool of myself about them like she does.*

She wished Uncle Jason was still living here. Jason and Stephanie had separated two months before Jessie's parents died, and now Uncle Jason was living on the other side of town. He never came near this house.

Before that, Marianne had been a lot easier to get along with, although she and Jessie had never been best buddies. For one thing, Jessie was a year younger. Worse, she was a notoriously well-behaved bookworm, while Marianne flocked with the butterflies.

30

Boys could be interested in me, why not? I'm not bad-looking.

Right. But next to Marianne you're nothing, whispered a voice in the back of her head. She's like a fire. People notice her. You're not even a match flame. You're the match*stick.*

And, Pete? Like I'd want Pete to be interested in me that way! Pete's my best friend! He's the brother I never had.

But he's not your brother. And, be honest. You're glad he's not.

Shut up!

She pushed those thoughts away, turned over to face the invisible ceiling, and thought about the empty attic above it.

How? How had he got out?

Nobody bigger than a baby could have got out that little window, or the matching one at the back. Even if Lucan could have squeezed through, which was impossible, it was three storeys to the ground. No way down unless he'd leaped like a squirrel to the maple's branches, and at that height they were too spindly to hold his weight.

Then how… well, duh! She got out of bed again. How he got out was obvious, when you thought about it. Still, she wanted to prove it to herself. *Don't think I could sleep, otherwise.*

She left her room and crept silently downstairs to the front door. The dead bolt would be open, of course. That had to be it. He'd snuck down while they were asleep and got out this way.

He panicked, I guess. I'll probably never see him again. An odd mix of relief and disappointment blew through her.

But, no. The dead bolt was shot, the way Steffie always left it. He hadn't got out this way.

Jessie checked the kitchen door next. The latch was turned and the chain was fastened.

She went around feeling at the latches of the windows. Kitchen, living room, dining room. Locked, locked, locked. Steffie made sure of that every night.

31

Last thing, Jessie went down into the spider-webbed, damp-smelling, shadowy basement, a place she disliked even on a sunny day. She checked the two small windows. Both were locked. There was no other way out.

Chapter 7
Blood for Supper

"ANYWAY, HE WAS there in the morning," Jessie said. "Up in the attic. He said he'd never left."

"So how come you and Marianne didn't see him?" Pete walked hunched, fists deep in his jacket pockets.

"He said he scrunched down in a corner and hid his face, and he was all in black clothes, so we just overlooked him."

"Well, maybe." Pete chewed his lip, thinking. "No, it still seems funny. You said the light was on."

"Yeah. But that must've been the way it was, because what other way was there?"

Jessie zipped up her jacket to the neck. A wind that felt like the back end of October was scouring McClure Street, spinning dust devils across the road and blowing flocks of starlings across the sky.

It was four o'clock on Wednesday afternoon, but thick clouds made it as dark as evening. Jessie snuffled the air. "There's rain coming."

Pete laughed. "What, you smell it?"

"Yeah."

"That's a first. Usually my sniffer is better than yours." He kicked away a flying newspaper. "You really think he's sick?"

"He sure looked sick when I saw him this morning, after the others left. At noon I went home and he looked worse. He still hadn't touched the food and all he wanted to do was sleep. He wouldn't even let me open the shutters. He said his eyes hurt."

She hadn't felt her normal energetic self today either, come to think of it. "I keep wondering if maybe I caught some bug from him. You know, when our blood got mixed, from those cuts. Suppose he really has some terrible disease?"

"Something bad enough to keep him locked up, you mean?" Pete shook his head. "You don't put a sick kid in a cage in the basement, you put him in the hospital! At least, that's what any normal father would do. But maybe Dr. Erasmus isn't normal."

"I wouldn't be surprised."

A block north of the high school they turned right on Mercy Street, where Aunt Steffie's house stood in a row of others like it, worn-out red-brick houses with trim painted sad brown or gloomy dark green.

The street's only beauty was a double row of chestnut and maple trees, a green tunnel in summer, a red-gold tunnel in fall. Right now the wind was ripping the canopy to shreds. Stray raindrops flicked at Jessie's face.

Crows swooped above the street, cawing. Jessie winced. Their jagged cries cut at her ears. "Ugly birds!"

"I wouldn't say that." Pete watched them settle. "They're interesting. Really smart, for birds."

"What's that they're picking at, on our lawn?" Jessie hung back. "Ugh, don't go near it!"

Pete made a run at the crows and they scattered, screaming. "Raccoon." He nudged the fluffy body with the toe of his sneaker. "Dog must've got it. Poor thing, not much left, is there?"

Jessie shivered. She looked up at the silver maple, then from the tree to the attic window. "I bet this was the raccoon that woke us up last night and nearly got Lucan caught." She looked at the remains and managed not to gag. "We'll have to get that taken away."

"No, leave it to the crows. It's their job to clean up."

The house was dark when they filed into the front hall and shut the door. It was too early to be so dark, even on a day like this. Jessie wondered why, until she looked into the living room and saw the drapes were closed. When she'd left for school after lunch, they were open. Somebody else must have closed them again. Marianne?

At the end of the hall, in the kitchen, someone moved in the semi-dark.

"Marianne? Why'd you close the curtains?"

She walked through into the kitchen as she spoke. Pete came in behind her. The venetian blinds over the window were closed tight.

Marianne wasn't there. Lucan stood at the kitchen table, his dark sweater and pants making his body almost invisible in the dimness. He was like one of those black light puppets, Jessie thought, where only the white parts show.

He held something cupped in his hands. The pale oval of his face turned toward them. "I got hungry."

Jessie left the light off but stepped over and twitched open the blinds. A gleam of watery daylight found its way through the clouds and lit up Lucan's hands.

He yelped, dropped his handful splat on the table, and raced for the stairs. In a moment his footsteps thudded over their heads. Back to the attic.

Just like a beetle scurrying back under its rock, away from the light. Jessie cringed, but the thought stuck. Pete flipped the light switch and they looked at the table.

Pete breathed in through his teeth. "Yowsers."

Jessie grabbed paper towels and groped under the sink for spray cleaner.

"What's wrong with him?" Pete was staying well back from the table.

"I don't know!" She scooped the pile of raw ground beef into a

35

plastic bag, dumped it beside the sink, then mopped and cleaned the splattered blood from the table and floor.

"Now," she said, as she washed her trembling hands. "We'll go up there and ask him."

Chapter 8
Bred in the Bone

"PORPHYRIA." Lucan hunkered at one end of the cot with his arms wrapped around his knees. The windows and shutters were closed and the light was off, but a little grey light filtered in through the cracks. Enough to show faces. Lucan's was as blank as a wiped chalkboard.

"Por what?" Jessie echoed.

"Never heard of it," Pete said flatly. He balanced on a stack of tied-up magazines near the other end of the cot. Jessie sat near him, on the cot, at the far end from Lucan. The stretch of blanket between themselves and him looked like a trackless desert.

"No wonder, it's rare. And don't worry, it's not catching." His eyes skipped from Pete's face to Jessie's.

"I wasn't worried," she said.

"Yes, you were."

Pete stirred. "Not catching, you said."

"It's genetic. That means it runs in the family."

"I know what that means, I'm not ignorant!"

"Right. My father has it, my grandfather had it, my children will probably have it. It doesn't kill you, just makes you miserable. You can't live a normal life."

"Is that why the light bothers you?" Jessie asked.

"Electric light doesn't bother me, except when it's really bright, but direct sunlight can make me sick."

"Gosh!" *Never to feel the sun on your face. Never to lie in the grass and just soak it in.*

He nodded at her. "It's like a bad, bad allergy. Night's the only time I feel really well. I feel halfway good on dark days like this. On a sunny day, I just sleep."

She had a feeling he was tiptoeing among facts, choosing which to tell and which to hide. Trying to decide which ones might scare them away. She wondered if he'd ever had any friends. Maybe not. That would explain why he talked in that grown-up way. He'd probably hardly ever been with kids his own age.

Sympathy stabbed her. She leaned over and touched his wrist and found it hot, the skin thin as silk. "We won't tell on you."

His eyes held hers. He almost smiled. "Thank you."

"But why the raw meat?" Pete demanded. "Why the heck would you want to eat that?"

"I wasn't eating it, I was … well … sucking it." Silence in the attic. "To get the blood."

The rafters creaked in a gust of wind. There was no other sound. Lucan let out his short, soft laugh. "I wish you could see your faces!"

Jessie cleared her throat. "You've got to admit it's, uh, unusual."

"Disgusting, you mean. Why do you think I was raised away from other people?" He added matter-of-factly, "It's all about my red blood cells. I don't have enough and I have to keep replacing them."

"A kind of anemia." Pete looked relieved.

"That's it. It's very rare, very hard to treat. Uncooked blood is one of the few foods I can digest."

"Oh." Jessie felt foolish. "Then, the pumpernickel and the cheese... "

"Can't eat them. Appreciated the thought, though."

"You should have told me!"

"I couldn't risk it. Didn't know how you'd react."

Pete's stack of magazines crackled. He glanced at the glowing dial of his watch. "I have to get home. Jessie, we gotta talk."

"In a minute. Look, Lucan, what about your father? Why did he put you in that cage?"

"Right," Pete said. "Now that you're telling the truth, why not tell it all?"

Jessie caught the hardness in his voice. She wondered how the boy who would pour his heart out for a hurt cat or a sick iguana could be so cold to one of his own kind.

Lucan's fingers whitened around his ankles. For a moment she thought he was going to jump up and hit Pete. Pete didn't change position but he went tight as steel wire.

The moment passed. Lucan's hands relaxed. "You know my father's a scientist. And I told you he's got porphyria too. He's been trying to find a cure."

Pete's head went up. "So that's why he has that lab full of animals?"

"Yes. He studies the biochemistry of regeneration."

"Right: lizards can re-grow parts of themselves, can't they?" Pete was suddenly fascinated. "And snakes grow new skins and shed the old ones. Cool!"

"Okay," Jessie said. "But why would he... " She drew a quick breath. "He couldn't!"

Lucan moved one shoulder, a minimal shrug. "He could."

"He was going to *experiment* on you?" Jessie could hardly get the words out. "Your own father?"

"He's afraid," Lucan said simply. "He's terrified of what this disease will do to him. You see, when you get old it gets into your brain. Think what that would mean."

Again they were silent. What must it mean to Lucan? Jessie wondered. Her chest ached and she realized it was her heart that was hurting.

"He's got hold of an idea that if he can, well, take me apart, to find out what's wrong with me... "

"Take you apart!" Pete exploded.

"Dissect," Lucan said. "Cut up. You know. Like one of his lizards."

Jessie couldn't move.

"He thinks he can find the cure in my blood and my brain. And... of course, this part is not scientific at all... he believes the phases of the moon are involved."

Another silence, while the wind shook the house. Very softly Lucan finished, "That's why he's so stuck on my sixteenth birthday, two days from now. It so happens there's a full moon that night. He told me the timing will be perfect. That's when he plans to kill me."

JESSIE GOT UP abruptly from the cot. "Be right back," she said, and climbed down the folding stairs. With Pete close behind she went down to the kitchen, opened the plastic bag of raw ground beef and poured the dripping mess into a clean white bowl.

She sniffed at it. "You know, I never noticed before, but fresh raw meat doesn't smell all that bad. It's got a sort of spicy smell."

Pete laughed. "Planning to slurp it up yourself?"

"Could if I wanted. There are places they serve raw steak as a gourmet food, you know. In France, right? Only they call it something else. And in Japan they eat raw fish."

"Not in Finnismore, they don't!"

Jessie decided to make this bizarre snack as delicious-looking as possible. While Pete looked on in amazement, she set the bowl on a red enamel tray with a folded linen napkin beside it. She got one of the good silver forks to lay on the napkin.

"What's the drink?" Pete whooped. "Beet juice?"

"Water should be safe." Jessie took one of Steffie's crystal tum-

40

blers from the dining room cabinet and filled it with mineral water.

"I'll go on Vic's computer tonight, if he'll let me," Pete said. Vic was his oldest brother. "I'll find out what I can about this porphyria. I never heard of anything so weird. D'you think he's telling the truth?"

"I think so. Mostly." An achy feeling pressed up into her throat. It felt like tears. *I'm not the crying type. What's got into me?*

"What's the matter?" Pete said.

"Nothing! Just... Pete, I'm so glad you stuck around. I mean, with all this." She waved at the tray, and up at the attic.

"Oh, well. Fair's fair. Remember the circus?"

She grinned, recalling the time last spring when Pete had persuaded her and a bunch of other kids from school to stage a sit-down demonstration in the Finnismore town council chamber. Council was about to vote on whether to let a live-animal circus set up in the fair grounds.

"Only two people actually showed up," Pete said. "Me and you."

"But it worked." She bounced her fist on his shoulder. "They voted No. We won!"

"Yeah. That was the best." Pete folded his arms. "But this guy! I still can't swallow what he says about his father. Dr. Erasmus is an important man, right? He couldn't be as crazy as all that without people knowing."

"Well, they do say he's strange." Jessie turned over in her mind everything she'd heard about Lucan's father. It wasn't much. "He's rich and he has this big, fancy house, but hardly anybody's ever been inside."

"He teaches a biology course at the university, but he never sees his students," Pete said. "He does it all online." He headed for the front door, where he'd left his book bag. "Seems like he hates people."

Jessie followed him, carrying the tray. She meant to carry it up to

41

the attic as soon as Pete left. "That's not so weird. Lots of people take courses online."

THE FEELING swept over her between one step and the next. A sickness in the stomach, a clutch at the heart. She forgot to breathe.

Fear. It picked her up and wrung her out. Keeping hold of the tray, not dropping it, took every ounce of her willpower. She bent to set it down on the floor. Then straightened up and stared at the door.

Pete swung his bag to his shoulder and reached for the doorknob.

"No!"

He looked at her, startled. "What? Why?"

"Don't go out!"

The bell rang. The sound knifed through her head.

"Aren't you going to answer it?" Not waiting for an answer, Pete opened the door.

The tall man on the doorstep wore a spotless beige raincoat, neatly buttoned against the rain. Cold air blew in around him.

"I am August Erasmus," he said. "I have come to take my son home."

Chapter 9

Dr. Erasmus

IN THE TIME it took for Jessie's heart to thump twice, nobody moved. Yes, she thought, there's a likeness. Tall, thin, with Lucan's sea-glass eyes. The delicate features aged to sharpness, the moon-silk hair a flat white.

She already knew what he looked like: she'd seen his photo in the newspaper. But in person, he was different. It was the difference between a magazine picture of a tiger and that same tiger standing over you, its yellow eyes gazing into yours, its teeth just beginning to show.

Pete moved. "Sorry, you've got the wrong house." He started to close the door, but Erasmus put a hand to the knob and gave it a gentle push, and Pete flew backward. His shoulder rammed the newel post of the stairs. He yelped with pain.

Erasmus smiled at him, a white knife-edge. "You're the boy who phoned in a complaint to the Humane Society this morning."

Pete pushed away from the newel post and squared his shoulders. Jessie grabbed his arm, but he shook her off. "They shouldn't have told you. It's supposed to be anonymous."

"But I asked nicely and they did tell me. You'll be happy to know that all my animals are being treated well. The Society, bless them, will have no reason to return to my house. Nor will you."

His eyes, hard on Pete's, narrowed and brightened. A shudder shook Pete from head to foot. He started to say something, but suddenly closed his mouth and stepped back. And then Jessie was out in front, face to face with the man who had locked Lucan in a cage.

Erasmus's eyes skimmed past her and fixed, and she knew he had spotted the tray, with its crystal glass and its bowl of raw meat. "How kind," he purred. The fine hairs stood up on the back of Jessie's neck.

Then he laughed. There was a vast amusement in the sound. "And how sad your kindness will go to waste." His eyes flicked up at the ceiling. He tilted his head as if to listen. "Yes, he's gone. I won't trouble you further."

Gone? Jessie wondered. How would he know?

Erasmus shook down the cuffs of his sleeves, turned to the door, then smoothly turned back. He caught Jessie's eyes before she had time to look away.

It hurt. She quivered like a butterfly on a pin.

Erasmus still smiled: a small, closed-mouth smile like Lucan's. "I knew your father. Clement Brown was a fine tradesman. The work he did for me was faultless. A pity he was such a busybody."

Anger flared through her. "My father was not a busybody!"

"Oh, yes. Couldn't mind his own business. And didn't know when to take a hint. But you're not like that, are you, Jessie?"

"I, I don't know what you're talking about."

"You're a smart girl. You'll know when to keep your nose out of other people's affairs. Hm?"

With an effort that felt like tearing her own flesh, she pulled her gaze away from his. He made a faint surprised sound, then moved, and when she looked again he was out the door and striding down the walk. A long, shiny white Cadillac waited at the curb.

Pete started to swing the door closed, but Jessie caught it. "Look. Who's that man out there?"

A man in a driver's jacket and peaked cap stood by the car, holding open the passenger door. Erasmus ducked in, the car door closed, the driver circled the car and got in and then they were on their way

44

with a whisper of tires on wet asphalt.

"Don't know him," Pete said. "Just a driver."

"He looked like that man in the bleachers, yesterday."

Jessie closed the door and rested her head on it. Why should a sight of the driver's face: bland, expressionless, grey, send such a chill down her spine? In his way, he scared her as much as Erasmus did.

"Do you think he was right?" she said. "Is Lucan gone?"

"Of course not." Pete rubbed his shoulder. "There's no back way out from the attic, except that little window. Lucan's still up there. The guy was just trying to mess with our heads, to make us give the game away. I think we did okay."

"Well, we'll see." Jessie stooped to pick up the tray. As she straightened up, the door flew open and Marianne barged in. Raindrops sprayed onto the wallpaper from her umbrella, which was pink with falling dogs and cats printed all over it.

"That was Dr. Erasmus, right? What was he doing here?"

"Oh," Jessie said. "He, um."

"He was asking directions," Pete put in.

"Why? Like, he lives in town. He knows it."

Jessie shrugged, but she had nowhere to hide the tray in her hands. Marianne made a face. "What's with that yuck?"

"I'm about to, uh, start dinner." That sounded believable, at least. She did cook sometimes. She'd learned some dishes from her mother, which was more than Marianne could say. "I'm making shepherd's pie."

"With Mom's good glassware and silver?"

"Why not?"

"Stupid idea." Marianne speared her umbrella at the umbrella stand, missed, and let it flop wetly to the floor. "Did you see that dead raccoon out front?"

"Sure did," Pete said.

"I bet that was what was running around in the attic last night. Running *from* something, I thought." Marianne kicked her fuchsia suede boots off into another corner. They were soaked with rain.

"You mean, from another raccoon?" Jessie asked, just to seem interested.

"Or whatever. And hey, what happened to it?" Marianne widened her eyes. "Hardly anything there but the fur and the bones. Isn't that gross?"

"I'm amazed you'd go near it." Jessie was tired of playing games. "Marianne, what are you after with this?"

"Oh, I don't know, it just seems so *sinister*." Marianne leaned close and hissed. "The poor little wrung-out corpse! The secret in the old attic!" She leaned back. "If I were you, I'd stay out of that attic. Who knows what's up there?"

She laughed, but it wasn't a playful laugh. Ill-will prickled up like a red rash all over her face. Jessie shook her head. *I didn't see that. You can't see things like that.*

Marianne scooped up her dripping boots. She dangled them on her fingertips. "Nice, eh? Cost two hundred bucks. My dad paid for them. Wait'll I show them to Mom!"

"And how good will that make her feel?"

Jessie knew it was the wrong thing to say the moment it popped out. The smile slid off Marianne's face. "None of your business!" She ran up the stairs. A door slammed.

Pete looked a question at her. "Weird how she hit all around the truth."

"She guessed last night that I was hiding somebody."

"But she can't know anything. It's like she's flailing around with her eyes closed, trying to hit something. What's eating her?"

"Trying to hit me. Don't ask me why."

Chapter 10

Slither

JESSIE LAY AWAKE, listening to her window rattling. It was an old six-paned window, and after eighty years every pane sat loose. When the wind gusted, they chattered like teeth.

What did he mean: my father a busybody? What business did he mind that wasn't his own?

At least she could guess what work he'd done for Dr. Erasmus. That lock on the silvery cage in the basement. Her father had repaired that lock. No, more likely he'd built it. He was that good. Had been that good. A master locksmith.

The more she thought about it, the worse she felt.

Maybe Dad had guessed the cage would be put to a bad use. Maybe he'd tried to tell the police. Maybe he'd even seen Lucan … no, that was out. Lucan had only come here a little while ago, or so he'd said. Dad died a year ago.

"Dad and Mom," Jessie said firmly, aloud. Strange, because she had loved them both. But Mom was the one who was beginning to fade from present pain into the softness of memory. Dad was the one who kept popping back into her mind, almost as if he was still alive somewhere. Prodding her, nudging her. To do what? Anyway, he hadn't faded.

The memory of how they'd died, and Jessie had survived, hadn't faded either. But she closed her mind against it, as always, and pushed it away.

Then, for almost the first time, she pulled it back and took a look at it. One look was enough. The figure flashing across the road, the swerve, the scream. And then blackness.

And then the part that always came into the dream. She wasn't sure if it had really happened, or if the dream had invented it. It was worse than the actual accident, though she couldn't say how. It was just a window, a round-cornered square with glass jagged along the bottom. And a face looking in. Smiling.

No.

Jessie sat up and pushed hard and made it go away again.

No use trying to sleep. If it wasn't bad dreams and bad memories, it was worry about Lucan. Where was he? Dr. Erasmus had been right (guessed right?): Lucan was gone again. When she'd carried the tray up to the attic, he wasn't there. Really not there, this time: she'd poked into every corner.

And then she'd had to go downstairs and make shepherd's pie.

How did he get out?

The luminous clock dial beside her bed said it was just after one a.m. She slid out of bed, shook her flannelette pyjama legs down from where they had scrunched around her knees, and went to the window.

Her room overlooked the back yard and the lane. There should have been nothing to see but blackness below. And above, the black shapes of roofs and wind-tossed trees against a sky of faintly glowing cloud.

But something was moving in the lane. I've been staring into the dark so long I've got my night eyes, Jessie thought. What is that? Man-size, and dressed in something that glistened, a wet plastic rain-coat, perhaps.

Didn't move like a man, though. It sort of … scuttled. Jessie had an image of a long, wiry body and short legs. She couldn't picture the face.

48

Her wondering was idle until the figure stopped at the point where Aunt Steffie's yard was divided from the neighbour's. It placed both hands on the fence and climbed... no, *slithered* over.

"It's coming here!" She backed away from the window, then darted forward for another look. There was no sign of whoever-it-was now. It must be so close against the house she couldn't see it from where she stood. It might be at the back door right this instant, prying at the lock.

For gosh sakes, don't just stand there! Wake Aunt Steffie!

She was halfway to the door of her room when a thin shriek sliced through the night. A scuffling and thumping broke out in the yard. When Jessie reached the window again, the fence was shaking as if something had leaped over it at top speed.

For a minute nothing moved in the dark below. Jessie stood with her face against the glass, her heart thudding.

Then, with a rush, her window darkened and a white face hovered inches from hers, smiling. She gasped and leaped back.

"Jessie, wait!" he called through the glass. "It's me!"

She stopped, looked. Something about his wide smile caught at the edge of her attention, but she found she couldn't look at his mouth, his eyes were so bright and full of laughter.

"Open up, Jessie," Lucan said. "Open up and let me in!"

She leaped forward again and yanked at the sash. Rain had swollen the wood, but she was able to tug it a few inches open and then Lucan, who had already pushed up the screen, got his fingers under the sash and pulled. It went up with a loud squeak, and he swung himself through.

"How'd you get up here?" She poked her head through the window. There was no drain pipe, no trellis, nothing to climb on. She craned her neck to look up. Same story: plain brick wall. The only thing up there was the rear attic window.

She pulled her head back into the room and looked for him. He stood almost invisible in the shadow beside the window. "Climbed! A hobby of mine, wall climbing. I'm really good at it." There was a laugh in his voice.

"Someone was out there. Did you see?"

"I chased it off. It won't be back tonight."

"But who was it?"

"One of my father's hired hands. Looking for me, no danger to you. Don't worry, Jessie." He touched her wrist with one dry, hot finger. "I won't let anyone hurt you."

Funny that he thought he was protecting her, when really it was the other way around. "Your father was here this afternoon."

"I know. I felt... I heard him. Looked out, saw the car. So I scrammed."

"But how?"

"Out the back window. Haven't you noticed how skinny I am?"

"Not that skinny." But other questions crowded that one out. "Is that how you plan to get back in the attic? Climb?"

"Sure. But later. I'm not tired yet."

"You must be hungry, though. When's the last time you ate?"

"Oh, about an hour ago."

"But where did you find food? I mean, you can't just go into Burger Queen and order a bowl of blood!"

He watched her with that secret smile. "Trust me." His voice brimmed with laughter. "I'm not hungry. I'm fine. And you know what else? I'm restless. I hate being cooped up. Come for a walk!"

"What, now? It's the middle of the night!"

"So? Come on, Jessie! How long has it been since you cut loose and just had fun?"

Funny how that stung, how mousy and boring it made her feel. She laughed, or tried to. "How would you know anything about that?"

"It's not hard to figure out." His shrug was barely visible. "You're all tied up in knots. Why take life so seriously? Believe me, it's too short!"

Chapter 11

Moon Magic

TEN MINUTES after Lucan ducked back out the window, Jessie eased the kitchen door shut, zipped up her windbreaker and crossed the yard to the gate. He was waiting in the lane.

"I just remembered," she whispered. "I haven't got my keys."

"Don't tell me you're locked out!"

"No, I left the latch undone. Should be okay." She looked along the lane both ways. "But suppose that guy comes back, that man of your father's? Suppose he gets in the house, and Aunt Steffie finds him, and... "

"Jessie! Relax!"

"But if he's still prowling around, it's too dangerous! For you, I mean!"

He laughed and caught her hand. "Will you stop worrying! Those guys are nothing. I can be more slippery than they can, when I put my mind to it."

"But... "

"Come *on*!" He set off running, her hand locked in his.

And not at an easy jog, either. Jessie pounded along the lane, somehow keeping her footing among the ruts and potholes. A puddle stretched ahead, a miniature lake, six feet if it was an inch. They leaped, cleared it with ease, and kept on running. Lucan whooped and Jessie heard herself laughing.

Then they were out on Mercy Street, skimming up the shiny black ribbon of road between the sleeping houses. They turned the corner onto King Street and sprinted on.

The town seemed deserted, even here. Almost all the shops were dimmed down for the night. Their two reflections darted and leaped across window after window, like a jerky old film. The more they ran, the more the urge to run burned in Jessie's bones.

"It's like we're flying!"

Lucan laughed a high, strange laugh and spread his arms and jumped, letting go of her hand, and for a moment she would have sworn he coasted on the air like a bird.

He hit the pavement with a smack and they were matching stride for stride again. They passed the all-night coffee shop at the corner of King and Iroquois Road. Jessie glanced into the bright interior. Startled faces gaped back at her.

Then they were into Jasper Street and angling across the baseball diamond. Damp turf bounced like rubber underfoot.

It was darker here, away from the lights of the commercial strip. But now she really had her night eyes. Each dip in the ground was plain to see, each grass blade sharp and distinct.

The world turned silver. Jessie looked up. The moon was bursting from torn clouds. It was slightly squashed on one side, like a pumpkin.

Lucan thudded to a halt beside her and gazed up at the moon. Its light caught like white fire in the streaming silk of his hair.

"Two nights until the full. Two nights until… " His lips pulled back in a snarl. Jessie's heart jumped. He looked at her quickly. "What's wrong?"

"Nothing. Just, for a sec there you looked… "

"Did I scare you? Sorry. That's the way my father affects me."

But there's something wrong with your teeth. She couldn't say it aloud. For one moment she was cold and breathless. Then Lucan's eyes caught hers and the fearful thought faded in their shine and laughter.

A few blocks away, a police siren started up. It was coming this way. Lucan tilted his head.

"There's a bite to the wind, isn't there? Come on, Jessie, let's warm our blood!"

They ran and ran. Across the park, over a head-high fence like two grasshoppers, through a row of back yards, hurdling hedges, flower beds, shrouded barbecues. Over the roofs of parked cars in giant leaps. A dog barked hysterically. In one house a window squeaked up and someone looked out. Lucan flashed a mocking grin upward and the window slammed shut. Jessie laughed.

This was the oldest part of town, a neighbourhood of sprawling Victorian houses and enormous maples and oaks and chestnuts. They were two flying shadows among the tree shadows. Jessie wasn't cold at all now. Her blood ran like warm honey in her veins. She could feel all the little rivers darting through her.

Another fence: a stone wall, this one. They sailed up and over. Wide spaces opened around them. A house stood just ahead, a boxy shape outlined in moon-silver, with a smaller third tier. Around the house spread a silvery lawn. To Jessie it looked half-familiar, but not quite real, like painted scenery on a stage.

"I sort of know this place. Where are we?"

"You should know it. You rescued me from that house."

"What? Lucan, you're crazy! Let's get out of here!" She backed toward the fence.

"Oh, come on." He strolled toward a flower bed, the one with the sundial in the middle. "There's no danger, not yet. My father's not home."

"How do you know?"

"I just know."

"But his hired men! They'll see you!" She looked at the house, its windows like rows of watchful eyes. She and Lucan were right out in the open. If anybody happened to glance out a window, it was game over.

"They won't see me if they're looking for me somewhere else, will they?"

"But I'd've thought you'd hate the place! Why did we come back here?"

"I want to show you something." He knelt down and used both hands to part the stems of the asters that crowded the sundial. "It's interesting. It's about my family."

She knelt beside him and helped him push the flowers aside. The moonlight found the pedestal. There, plain to see on the stone column, were the four figures she'd noticed when she used the aster patch as a hiding place. The two circles, one pale and one dark, with a semi-circle and a crescent between them.

"These are the phases of the moon. The full, the half, the last quarter. And the dark." Lucan ran his fingertips over the carvings. "You see, Jessie, it's not a sundial. It's a moondial."

"Moondial? But how could that work?"

"It's complicated. My father showed me this the first night he brought me here, before he put me in the cage. He explained a few things to me. Like, why the moon is special to us."

"I don't understand." Jessie felt cold again. The night's magic had drained away. It struck her that this midnight run was the kind of thing that would seem on the crazy side of wild when you woke up the next morning and thought about it by the plain light of day. And running straight back into the danger zone was not a completely sensible thing to do.

But then, "sensible" and Lucan didn't have much in common.

He let the asters sway up to cover the pedestal. Then he lay back on the damp grass, spread out his arms, and gazed up at the moon.

55

His eyes were like two more moons. "People like me, porphyrics, we can't bear the sun. It's poison to us. But we need energy, just like anybody else. Your energy comes from the food you eat and from the sun, right?"

It almost made sense. Jessie sat on her heels beside him, and thought. "But the moon reflects the sun."

"That's right! Now, listen." Still lying flat on his back, he waved a finger at her. "This is how it works. We porphyrics, our bodies are so sensitive, we soak up energy like sponges. And we spend a lot, so we need a lot. Well, the sunlight that reflects off the moon is one energy source. And the closer the moon gets to the full, the more moonlight there is: so, the stronger we feel."

Jessie managed a shaky laugh. "Sounds spooky."

He laughed too and flipped to his feet in one motion, like an acrobat. Jessie followed him up, slower. Then Lucan's smile went crooked.

"Imagine what people thought in the old days, before they knew about porphyria. I mean, imagine what ignorant people thought of us. What with the moon, and the blood, well... "

Her heart kicked her breastbone. *Vampires.*

Lucan held her eyes and nodded. "It's been in the family since 1567. Gabriel Erasmus, somewhere in the Netherlands, he was the first of us." His mouth twisted. "I sometimes wish he'd been the last." He kicked the moondial's pedestal, then turned away.

Jessie followed him. "But then you'd never have been born. You couldn't want that."

"Couldn't I? You don't know what it's been like. Always alone. I once heard of a man, a porphyric, who got sick of his life and decided to end it. Know how he did it?"

She shook her head.

"Simple. He went out in the sun. Killed him within the hour.

56

Roasted him like a turkey. I've sometimes thought of doing that."

"Lucan." She held out her hand, the one with the healed cut. He looked at it a moment, then slowly curled his fingers around it. She tightened her grip. "You're not alone! Don't ever think that."

"You mean it? Really?" He stepped closer.

"Of course, really!"

"If you really, really mean it... "

"Well, what?"

"It's just that I'm going to have to ask you for help again, soon. And this time I'm afraid you'll say no."

"Don't be so mysterious! What is it?"

"I'm going to need help facing my father."

"But I thought you didn't want to see him again." Strange how his eyes caught the light of the moon even when it was behind him. Almost as if they shone with their own light.

"He's still my father," Lucan said. "I have to have things out with him. I can't just go away without a word."

Jessie nodded. She could understand that.

"And when I do, I'll need a friend with me."

She thought of how Dr. Erasmus's eyes had skewered her the way a pin pierces a captured moth. Her insides curled up at the idea of letting those eyes get at her again.

But it had to be ten times worse for Lucan. *Having a father who wants to dissect him!*

"Okay! I said I'd help and I will."

His eyes brightened. "Do you swear?"

"Swear?" Suddenly she felt she was being hustled somewhere at breathless speed. She dropped his hand and took a step back. "Lucan, I'm your friend. If I say I'll do it, I'll do it. You don't need me to swear."

He showed both palms. "I'm sorry! I got anxious. I guess I don't know much about being a friend. I never had a friend, not a real one. Do you know what it feels like to be with someone who understands, for the very first time?"

"I know what it's like to be lonely."

"I guess you do. Jessie, I... There's something I should tell you." He looked at her, then at his hands. For once he seemed unsure of himself.

She punched his arm gently. "You have some other horrible secret?"

"It's about you, actually. I just don't know how to tell you."

"About me? What could you know about me that I don't know?"

If they'd had another minute, he might have told her. Later, she wondered how things would have turned out, if she'd discovered the truth right then. Would it have changed anything?

But he never did tell her. A sound rose on the wind: a whistling squeal that came from the direction of the house.

They froze and the call came again. Then again, this time from near the gate.

"What the heck *is* that?" Jessie spun, looking in all directions.

Lucan growled in his throat. "Hounds. Like the one that was in your yard."

She stood still. "But you said that was a hired man."

"Hound, man, same thing."

"But they can't be!"

The whistle came again, and now it had an eager, excited edge. "Just one was no problem," he muttered. "Now it's the whole filthy nest of them. Let's go!"

Chapter 12

The Hound

THEY BOUNDED across the lawn hand in hand, leaping flower beds. Jessie grabbed a glance over her shoulder and caught a flicker of wet raincoats near the house.

One of the shiny coats fell to hands and knees and started running across the lawn on all fours. It made terrifying speed. Jessie's stomach lurched and she stumbled.

"Keep going!" Lucan yanked at her hand. They crashed in among the bushes and squirmed into the gap between the poplars and the wall. She gasped up at its height.

"I can't climb that!"

"You can!" He grabbed her by the waist and hoisted. She shot into the air and threw her arms over the top of the wall. Another shove, and she was lying flat on top.

"Now," he said. "Get over that wall, and get home. I'll lead them away."

"I can't leave you here!"

"I won't get caught! But I can't do it with you along. You'll slow me down."

"But I can't just dump you!"

"Go!" His eyes flared at her, then the poplars thrashed and he was gone. She lay flat on top of the wall. Half a minute later, his whoop sounded an amazing distance away. The whistling calls rose in answer. Then they faded, and Jessie was alone in the moonlight.

She slid off the wall and landed on the grass outside, between two lilac bushes. Now, better get home. But she still stood there. It seemed wrong to desert Lucan now. Never mind that it was his fault, that his own craziness had brought them back to this place.

I'll wait a bit and listen. He might need help.

Clouds swallowed the moon. Darkness drowned the street. The houses slept, all lights out. The one street lamp made a distracting orange pool half a block away. It robbed Jessie of her night eyes. She found she could only see properly if she turned her back on the light.

Once her eyes were used to the dark again, she found a thick broken branch under the lilacs. She picked it up and waved it around. How much damage could it do? Probably not much, but it was better than nothing.

A rustle on the other side of the wall, a scrabbling noise. It might be Lucan. Or not. She gripped her ragged club.

It slid over the wall and dropped in front of her, landing in a crouch. Then uncurled to its full height. It wasn't Lucan. Not any kind of hound, either. It looked like a man, but distorted. Whatever it was, it reeked.

It was close to seven feet tall, stoop-shouldered, short-armed, with a narrow head. Its eyes were black buttons sunk in bony sockets. Its coat was an iridescent green-purple-black something wrapped around its spindly body.

Jessie never took in all the details, because she was looking at the thing's mouth as it darted at her. A wide, lipless mouth rimmed with teeth like needles. And a tongue that slipped in and out, in and out. On the tongue's tip a drop of wetness hung and gleamed.

This isn't real. This is a dream. Wake up!

It was the drop of wetness that stank. She knew it without knowing how. And she knew the reek was poison.

It darted again. The tongue flicked at her face. She jumped back, shielding her eyes with one arm, and swung her branch with the other

60

hand. It broke over the stone-hard skull and left her holding a stub of wood.

She hurled the stub at the jaws, turned and ran for the street. Something snagged her heel and sent her sprawling, sliding on her stomach over the grass.

She pulled her legs under her and was halfway up and ready to sprint when shoes hit the grass behind her. Then came a whistling shriek and a snapping, crackling noise, like a bowlful of eggs being crushed.

Jessie turned around, breathing hard now that she remembered to breathe at all. A tangle of shiny limbs was dragging itself under the lilac bushes. Lucan stood there and watched it disappear.

"What did you do to that thing?" She swallowed.

"I gave it something to remember me by."

"It looked broken." For a moment, the violence of what he had done scared her more than the creature itself.

"The vermin forgot its place and tried to bite me!" He slipped an arm around her. "Forget that thing. Anyway, that's enough fun for one night. It's only your first, after all."

"But, Lucan!" The strangeness of it hit her. She slid from under his arm and backed away from him. "What *was* that?"

"I told you," he said impatiently. "It was one of my father's men."

"It didn't look much like a man. It didn't look really human. It looked like, like... " Like something she'd seen not so long ago and not so far from here. Why couldn't she remember? "What's happening to my head?"

"Hey, easy. You're shaking!" His arm went around her shoulders again and his voice grew soft and soothing. "Of course he's human. What else could he be?"

"But his horrible tongue! And you said he tried to bite you."

She felt his shrug. "I meant hit, of course. He's deformed, by the way. My father hires people who can't get jobs anywhere else, because of the way they look."

"Why? Because he's so kind-hearted?"

Lucan laughed. "No, because he likes them strange."

That, at least, sounded true. And it was the only explanation that fit the facts, and still made a kind of daylight sense. After all, the man had to be human. What else could he be?

But as they walked home through the windy darkness, she wondered why she was so sure Lucan was lying.

LUCAN LEFT HER in front of the house. "I have things to do," he said. "I'll be in later." He was gone before she could ask him what things he could possibly have to do in the middle of the night.

She cut around by the lane and in through the back gate. Her first warning of trouble came when she tried to open the kitchen door. The knob wouldn't turn. It was locked.

But I left the thumb latch undone.

Somebody giggled.

Rats. "Marianne?"

The window beside the door was open half an inch. Marianne was kneeling behind it, laughing through the gap. "Wait 'til Mom finds out you broke curfew!"

"Marianne, will you unlock the door, please?"

"I love it! Little Miss Perfect, way way *way* past curfew!"

"I'm tired, Marianne. Come on. Open up."

"Okay, I'll let you in and I won't tell Mom." Marianne grinned through the gap. "If you tell me who you've been out with."

"What d'you mean?"

"You've been out with a boy. On a date. Right?"

"Wrong."

"Sure you were. And you're too young. Mom says I can't have a boyfriend 'til I'm sixteen, so why should you? Who is it? Tell!"

Jessie shook her head. She'd promised Lucan she'd keep his secret. A promise is a promise, her dad used to say. Don't make one if you're just going to break it.

She made a sudden dart at the window, but Marianne was ready. The window slammed shut. Marianne leaped up and twisted the latch. She smirked at Jessie through the glass. *Tell*, she mouthed.

Jessie flopped down on the cold, damp grass and looked up at her own window, twelve feet above her head. It was still wide open and the screen was still up. *Great. My room'll be full of moths and beetles and things.*

The kitchen window squeaked up. "I'll give you five minutes." Marianne held up the digital timer that usually sat on the fridge. "Then I'll tell Mom." The window banged down again.

Amazing how Lucan got up there, Jessie thought. But then, he truly was amazing, the things he could do. Wall-climbing!

There was a rock-climbing wall at the Finnismore Community Centre, but that was easy. Not like this. No handy bits of rock here, sticking out in just the right places. Nothing but flat bricks. You'd need a ladder.

A ladder. Jessie narrowed her eyes. Hadn't she seen an old wooden ladder around here somewhere?

Marianne tapped on the glass. She showed the digital timer again and held up four fingers.

Jessie jumped up and went over to the fence on the east side of the yard. Yes! Lying against the base of the fence, blanketed with morning glory vines, almost impossible to see in the tangle of moonlight and shadow: a ladder.

She ripped the vines away, dragged the ladder out, carried it across the lawn and propped it up against the wall. Perfect! The top

63

rung almost reached her window.

She started up. Halfway up she stopped to grin down into Marianne's flabbergasted face, flattened on the glass. Marianne ducked away. Jessie laughed and climbed on. So this was how he'd reached her window. No mystery, no super skills. The ladder!

No, wait a minute. She stopped, just short of her window, and leaned on the rungs. Lucan hadn't used this ladder, you could see that by looking at the morning glories. The ladder hadn't moved from that spot since last spring.

"So how did he do it?" Jessie asked herself aloud.

She never worked out the answer, because just then Aunt Steffie's head popped out of the window. "Jessie! What on earth?" Marianne smirked from behind her shoulder.

Chapter 13

Sound and Fury

"IT COULD HAVE BEEN a lot worse," Jessie told Pete the next day. They were eating lunch in the school cafeteria. That is, Pete was eating. Jessie was pushing twists of torn paper napkin into her ears.

"So you're not grounded? I would've been."

"Aunt Steffie just lectured me for about ten minutes on acting responsibly and being mature and needing my sleep. But if it happens again, she'll lower my curfew to eight o'clock for a month."

"Fair." Pete slurped up another spoonful of bean and bacon soup.

"Yeah, but Marianne hit the ceiling." Jessie waved her hands wildly, Marianne-like. "She was all, 'That's it? That's it? If it was me the sky would fall!'"

"And would it?"

"No. Aunt Steffie's been really easy on her since Uncle Jason moved out. She hates me, Marianne does, that's all. Ever since I moved in there, she's hated me."

"Maybe she just hates sharing." Pete clanged his spoon into his empty soup dish.

Jessie winced. Today everything seemed too loud, even through the makeshift earplugs. The clatter of trays hurt her ears. The tangle of voices, the laughter, the cafeteria's cheerful uproar scraped her nerves raw.

"Sharing what? What does she ever share with me? She's a spoiled brat." She rubbed her arms, cold even under a thick sweater, and yawned until her jaws cracked.

65

"A bathroom, a TV, a kitchen, a breakfast table. A whole house, really." Pete unwrapped a ham and cheese sandwich and took an enormous bite.

"I wonder if that's it." She looked over at the window, where Marianne and her two best pals, Naomi and Lesley, monopolized the middle table. They were the loudest group in the place.

"Why don't you ask her? You know, clear the air."

"I should." Jessie watched the three of them giggling with their heads together. The hard part would be getting Marianne alone. Even harder, getting her to stop and listen.

"Tutor!" Marianne shrieked. Her two friends jumped. Heads turned. She leaped up, grabbed her book bag and ran out the door.

Jessie pressed palms to her temples. "Can't she do anything quietly?"

"Never mind, there's your chance." Pete pointed his sandwich at the doorway.

"Yeah, I guess." Jessie pushed back her chair and climbed painfully to her feet.

"Better hurry."

"I am hurrying!"

Jessie didn't dawdle, but she didn't race, either. A fast walk was the best she could manage. She would never have caught up if Marianne hadn't been trying to read a notebook while running, and tripped and dropped it, and dropped her book bag, and spilled papers all over the corridor floor.

Jessie helped her pick them up. "Here." She held out a handful of math problem sheets. Marianne muttered and stuffed them in her bag. She hoisted it to her shoulder and strode on.

"I need to talk," Jessie gasped behind her, out of breath.

"No time." Marianne hung a sharp right at the stairs and took them two by two.

Jessie fumed. It almost balanced out feeling sick. She floundered up the stairs. By the time she reached the top Marianne was out of sight, but where she'd gone was no mystery. Mr. Halasz was the math tutor. When Jessie dragged herself to his door, Marianne was standing outside, waiting for Mr. Halasz to finish with another math-challenged student.

"Why?" Jessie said. It was all she had breath for.

Marianne stared at her coldly. "Why what?"

"Why... do you... hate me?"

"I don't. Couldn't care less."

"Not true. You hate me." Jessie filled her lungs again. "Why?"

Marianne's stare turned hot. "You really want to know? Like, really? Here and now?"

"Ye... yes... "

"Okay, if you really, really want to know, it's because you're a sly bitch and you've been trying to steal my mother." She nailed her gaze to the window in the tutor's door.

"Sly... steal... " Jessie shook her head, then wished she hadn't. She clutched it with both hands. "Ow. How the heck could I steal your mother?"

Marianne turned her back. "Go away. No time."

Jessie walked around in front of her so she could see into her face. Yes, fuming really did help. "No, really. Tell me. How does a person do that, steal somebody's mother?"

Marianne smiled. For about half a second Jessie thought she was going to make a joke of it. Then she dropped her book bag with a crash. She held up her right hand. "One!" She stuck up her forefinger. "You're so good, you're revolting. Only you aren't really, are you. You're faking it, trying to get on my mother's good side, which is totally not necessary because she's always thought you're the perfect daughter!"

"What d'you mean, faking?"

"Two!" Marianne added a finger. She shook them in the air. "Your room. Never a pair of jeans on the floor, never an apple core on the desk. You make your bed before *breakfast*, for cripes sake!"

"So I'm not a slob. That's just me. You could try it."

"Three!" Marianne uncurled her ring finger and stuck it up. "You're so darn helpful!" Her voice rose. "You do the dishes without even being asked! You wipe around the bathroom sink when you're finished! You cook soup for my mom when she comes home tired!"

"You could do that! Instead of snarking at her all the time!"

"Four! Perfect student!" Marianne yelled. She unbent her little finger. "Always got your homework done on time! Never miss a day of school! Never fake being sick!" Her hand dropped. Her mouth sagged. "Face it, you're the daughter she wants. Not me." Marianne's voice fogged up, and for a moment Jessie thought she might cry. Then she shook her head hard and put on a sneer. "You even *look* like her. That's five!" She stuck her thumb in the air.

"I can't help how I look!"

"Shut up! Don't you get it? It used to be just my mom and dad and me. Now my dad's gone, and my mom's hardly ever home, and every time I turn around I fall over you, and it's like it's not even my own house any more! I hope you're happy with that!"

"Happy!" A wave of white fire roared through Jessie's head. She'd never known rage like this. She couldn't speak or think or see or hear. One tiny corner of her mind cowered, terrified. The rest was set to claw Marianne's face off.

Marianne took a sudden step back. The door swung open. Mr. Halasz stood there frowning. "Hey! People are trying to learn in here. Take your fight someplace else!"

"I have an appointment." Marianne slipped a look at Jessie (that wasn't fear, couldn't be!) and tried to edge in behind him.

"Oh, yes. Marianne Malloy. Well, come in. Unless you'd rather stand out here and scream." He marched back inside. Marianne started to follow him. Jessie caught her by the elbow. Marianne swung around and backed away.

The white fire had died, leaving Jessie empty. "Your parents are alive," she said. It was the only thing left to say. The only thing that mattered.

Chapter 14

A Green Fog of Hostility

"WELL, THAT DIDN'T take long. How'd it go?"

"Horrible. I made things worse." Jessie slumped into a chair and dropped her head on the table. "This whole day's a disaster. I wish I'd never got out of bed this morning."

"Why did you?"

"There was that French test. I probably just squeaked through."

Pete looked her over critically. "You look terrible."

"Thanks a lot!" *No more midnight runs for me.* Jessie lifted her head, then wished she hadn't. It hadn't stopped throbbing since she'd chased Marianne up the stairs.

"Hope you haven't caught something from Lucan." Pete unwrapped a mint-chocolate Nanaimo bar. "I did a search. Whatever he's got, I don't think it's porphyria."

Jessie inspected the tuna sandwich she'd bought. She nibbled off one tiny corner, grimaced, and put the sandwich down. It hardly tasted like food. "What did you find out?"

Pete pulled a handful of printed sheets from his book bag. "Take a look. Doesn't sound much like what Lucan told us. See that?" He spread out the papers and tapped a paragraph that was highlighted in yellow.

"'Rare genetic disorder,'" Jessie read. "'Low red blood cell count... severe sensitivity to sunlight... ' Sounds like Lucan to me."

Pete reached over her arm and picked up the sheets. "There's this bit. 'As the condition advances, the sufferer's appearance grows increasingly morbid. Discoloration of the skin and an unusually thick growth of body hair can develop. Skin lesions form and spread, eventually attacking bone and causing severe facial deformity.' So, they turn into ugly, hairy monsters. That doesn't sound like Lucan, does it?"

"No."

"Or even Dr. Erasmus, and he must've had it longer. And there's more. If they really had porphyria, they'd have brown teeth and nails." Pete slapped the papers down on the table.

"So what does that add up to?" Jessie rubbed her aching forehead.

"He was lying. I think we should tackle him on it. Find out what's really going on."

"Look, tomorrow's, um. Friday. His birthday." She closed her eyes. *So tired I can hardly talk!* "Just one more day. Don't pick on him. Okay?"

"Pick on him?" Pete looked astonished.

"You never liked him. Not since he killed that gerbil. Even though that was an accident."

He scowled at her. And she knew then she was right about how he'd never liked Lucan. She could almost smell it, almost see it, an acid green fog of hostility all around him, as if it was oozing out of his pores.

I'm seeing things. I really must be sick!

"It's not just the gerbil." Pete was still scowling. "I don't trust him. I don't think he's been honest with us. I don't think you should trust him either."

"That's for me to say, right?"

His face closed down. She expected him to pick up his papers and walk away, but he just stuffed the rest of the Nanaimo bar in his face and chewed. The amount he ate made her feel ill.

71

"All right. We'll ask him. Again." She got up from the table. "Come to my place after school."

She went to the school nurse and very soon after that was on her way home with orders to rest and take fluids and not spread her germs, whatever they were, to anybody else.

Chapter 15

Truth and Sausage

LONG GOLDEN beams of sun lanced along Mercy Street as Jessie opened the door. She ducked back from the glare, pulled Pete in by the sleeve and slammed the door. "It's nearly supper time! What took you so long?"

"Science Club. It's every Thursday, you know that. Where's Lucan?"

"I looked in on him just now. He's sleeping."

"We'll just have to wake him up, then," Pete said briskly.

"Mom?" A bright, cheerful voice piped up at the inner end of the hallway.

Jessie could have kicked herself. She'd forgotten to find out where Marianne was. She turned around. Marianne stood in the doorway to the kitchen, holding a spatula. Jessie looked again. A spatula? Marianne?

"Oh, it's you." She flashed a smile, startling Jessie again. "Hi there, Pete."

"Hi." Pete waved.

"Pete's come over to, uh, do homework with me," Jessie said. She sniffed the air. "Something's burning."

"Oh, crap!" Marianne whirled away.

"I've got to see this," Jessie said.

"Take it easy on her," Pete said behind her, but she wasn't listening. She was in the kitchen, looking around with both hands to her mouth.

The room was a mess. It looked as if every pot and cutting board they owned was out. Scrunched-up paper towels and onion skins littered the floor. Tomato innards puddled on the table. A cheese grater stood up to its ankles in a pile of grated (Jessie sniffed) parmesan. A pot on the stove was bubbling. A saucepan was smoking.

"Mom's coming home early, so I'm cooking dinner. Spaghetti. From scratch!" Marianne pointed the spatula at a cookbook propped up on the windowsill, then went over to the stove and started poking at some blackened scraps in the saucepan.

"You're kidding." Jessie couldn't help it.

"You want a hand?" Pete asked.

"No!" She spun around. "*I'm* cooking, I said! Look, I bought all the stuff, the tomatoes and sausage and green pepper and garlic and the pasta and this really hard Italian cheese, and I've cut stuff up and now I'm browning stuff." She did a little kick dance from the table to the counter. "It's going to be spectacular!"

Jessie coughed. A thick haze hung under the ceiling. She picked up a bottle. "Oh, no wonder. This is olive oil. This burns if you heat it too high." She reached for the dial on the back of the stove.

Marianne slapped her hand away. "Back off! I know what I'm doing!"

"But it's burning!"

The word was hardly out when a shriek ripped the world open. It knocked Jessie to the floor. She jammed hands over her ears and squirmed under the table, but that was no shelter. She had a vague view of Pete opening the window and Marianne doing something at the stove, but nothing made sense. Her head was in pieces. Her brain was mush.

It stopped. She lay shaking, trying to hear past the ringing in her ears. Pete's worried face appeared above her. "What was that?" she whispered.

74

"Just the smoke alarm. I disconnected the battery."

"Wow." Marianne was on hands and knees, looking in from the other side of the table.

"She's sick," Pete said.

"It's doing funny things to my ears." Jessie sat up and bumped her head on the underside of the table. "Ouch! They're super-sensitive." She crawled out, leaned back against the table leg, and clasped her knees. She didn't feel ready to get up and walk.

"I turned down the heat on the onions. Maybe they were getting a little dark." Marianne settled on the floor cross-legged. "Okay, this is it, right?"

"It? What?"

Marianne's cheeks went bright red. "What you said today at school. I've been thinking. We should get this junk out of the way." She inspected her fingernails. "Might as well do it now."

"Yeah, now's good," Jessie said, though she wasn't sure what was coming.

Pete started climbing to his feet. "I'll go."

"No!" Jessie pulled him back down. She felt she might need him.

"Oh, it's okay." Marianne studied Jessie's left sneaker. "See, it's like this. When my parents split up, I was mad at everybody. I was mad at them, I was mad at myself. I hated the whole world. And then you came along. My dad was gone, and there you were instead. And everything was wrecked."

"But your dad left *before* I came."

"I know, I never said it made sense. You were somebody to hate besides myself. Wait, I have to cut the sausage." She got up.

Jessie remembered that time. They'd been two huge silences. Her own silence like a dark cave that she crawled into. Marianne's silence like a big steel ball studded with sharp spikes. And poor Aunt Steffie fluttering around between them trying to make things better.

Only one thing had made anything better. One person. Pete. He'd walked Jessie to school every day. He'd been there when she finally crawled out of her cave. He'd known when she wanted to talk and when she wanted everybody to just shut up.

I suppose he thought of me as a sick gerbil. She smiled at him. He wrinkled his forehead at her.

And in all that time Marianne hadn't really come out from inside her spiky steel ball. Even with all those friends she had. Maybe they weren't very good friends. *Well, she didn't have Pete.*

She didn't have me, either. The thought surprised her. But once it was out, it wouldn't go away.

Marianne sat down on the floor again with a cutting board and sharp knife and several thin smoked sausages. "Okay, I can't blame you for my parents splitting up. I don't, really. I mean, that would be stupid." The knife flashed. "And I'm sorry about your mom and dad. I *am*. That must be really bad."

"Yeah. It is."

"And I don't suppose you're actually trying to steal my mother." *Chop chop chop!* "It just seems like that sometimes."

"No. I like Aunt Steffie but, well, she can't take Mom and Dad's place."

"I totally get that." Marianne pushed aside a pile of sausage. It was minced nearly to atoms. She started on the next one.

"And I get it about your parents," Jessie said. "That's rough."

Marianne made a grim noise.

"But you know, I don't actually look like your mom." Marianne shot her a narrow look. Jessie nodded. "It's true. I look like my dad, everybody says so. Aunt Steffie's his sister, so no surprise if she looks kinda like him too." She risked touching Marianne on the wrist of her knife-wielding hand. "You look a lot like your dad." And she did: Uncle Jason was tall and red-haired, and he walked with a bit of

76

a swagger. Just like Marianne. *I guess that means she can't help it, the way she is.*

Marianne let the blade rest. She smiled. "Yeah." She ran a greasy hand through her long curls, then made a face at her fingers. "I wish... No, I don't wish." She picked up the knife and attacked the next sausage. "I *know* he'll come home. One of these days. They just have to get talking." She pointed the knife at herself. "That's what I've been doing, you know. I talk to Mom about Dad. And I talk to Dad about Mom. I do that every chance I get."

"You think that'll make them want to get back together?"

"I don't know. But it's the only thing I can do. It's, like, my mission. Not to let them forget each other."

I'd like to help. The words were on the tip of her tongue, about to jump off. She swallowed them. Marianne wouldn't welcome the offer. Instead she said, "Hope it works out."

"It will. It has to." Marianne poked at her heap of pulverized sausage. "Lookin' good." She got up and carried the cutting board to the counter, then turned on the radio. Rap music came hammering out of it. She turned up the volume. Jessie flinched.

"You okay now?" Pete stood up and held down a hand. "Don't forget we've got homework."

"Homework. Right." She grabbed his hand and pulled herself up. "Marianne? You sure we can't help? With dinner, I mean."

"No way! It's my mess, all mine."

"Okay." Jessie headed for the door.

"Oh, and Jessie."

"Yeah?" She turned.

Marianne was frowning. "Look, we're cool now, right? But don't expect us to be best buddies. I'm not even sure I like you. You're such a goody."

"Oh, thanks."

77

Marianne flipped a pot holder. "I know you can't help it. But that's why I was kind of glad when I thought you might be messing around. It made you, like, almost human." She sighed. "What'll I do now when I feel crappy? Who am I gonna dump on? It has to get out somehow, or I swear one of these days I'll explode."

"You could join the tae kwon do class at the community centre," Pete said. "That way you'd get to hit and kick lots of people."

"Yeah, that would be good. Maybe I'll do that. I'll get Lesley and Naomi to sign up with me. I could kick them."

While they were talking, the local news had come on. Marianne reached to change the station. Her hand stopped on the dial.

"...blood," the reporter was saying. "It happened at a dairy farm east of Finnismore. The farmer, Amos Martin, heard a commotion in his cowshed last night, around midnight. On investigating, he found one of his cows wounded in the neck, as if someone had been drawing blood from the animal. Police will not rule out a mutilation cult similar to... "

Marianne turned the radio off. "Sick!" she said. "And weird." She looked across the kitchen. "Who would do a thing like that? I hope it's not anybody in town."

Pete made a scornful sound. "'Course not!" But underneath his scorn he was afraid, Jessie could feel it.

She thought of Lucan, last night, a little after one o'clock. Not hungry, he'd said: ate an hour ago. And then the brightness, the energy, the secret laughter in his eyes.

AUNT STEFFIE came home just then. She stopped in the kitchen doorway. Her briefcase thudded to the floor. "Oh good lord."

"I'm *trying* to make dinner," Marianne said. "I'm doing fine. It wouldn't look like this if you'd been here to cook. Which would be nice once in a blue moon."

"Oh, Marianne." Aunt Steffie sighed and picked up a sponge.

Marianne turned her back and disappeared into a cell phone conversation. "Hi, Dad. How ya doin'? Going out? Want to take me out too? Aww... "

She wandered around the kitchen talking loudly into the phone. Steffie made a lot more noise than she normally would, banging cupboard doors and clanging pots and gushing water into the sink.

Jessie retreated back along the hallway. "We're going up to study," she called to the clangour in the kitchen. She led Pete up the stairs. "Make noise," she murmured. They tramped their feet on the stairs and in the hallway above, and then she opened the door of her room, paused, and slammed it shut.

Then they tiptoed along the hall to the closet and pulled down the stairs with the faintest of squeaks. With the closet door closed behind them, they climbed silently to the attic. They left the stairs unfolded below.

Pete reached for the light chain but Jessie pulled his hand down. "No, somebody might see."

"But *I* can hardly see. Where is he?"

"Over there." She pointed into the darkest corner. Not that it was very dark, to her eyes. The sun was on the edge of the world, and enough of its light seeped through the cracks in the shutters to fill the dusty space with a soft, rosy glow.

"Where?" Pete stumbled over a stack of magazines and raised a cloud of dust. He sneezed.

Patiently, Jessie led the way to where Lucan had built a wall of cardboard boxes to protect his sensitive eyes. The folding cot was behind the boxes, with the attic roof sloping down on the other side. Lucan lay on the cot in a cocoon of blankets, not a hair showing.

The two of them squeezed into the narrow space around the cot. Jessie pulled back a flap of blanket and uncovered Lucan's face. One hand was spread over his eyes. She touched his wrist, then snatched her hand back.

"He's icy cold!"

"Maybe he really is sick," Pete said.

"Lucan?" Jessie called softly. He still slept.

"Lucan! Wake up!" Pete grabbed the limp hand, then dropped it. "Yikes!"

Scared, Jessie gripped Lucan by the shoulders and shook him. His head flopped back and forth.

Pete pulled her away. "That won't help! Let me." He pressed two fingers firmly on Lucan's thin wrist below the thumb.

Half a minute went by, then a minute. Jessie held her breath. Her heart bumped. Pete's eyes grew larger and darker. Very carefully, he laid Lucan's hand back on the cot.

Jessie thought she'd explode. "Well?"

Pete drew a breath. "He's got no pulse."

"What?"

"He's dead."

Chapter 16

Monster

BECAUSE JESSIE was staring wide-eyed at Lucan's face, she caught the moment. It came just as the rose light chilled to ash.

The sun was suddenly gone. Her head cleared and a weight lifted from her spirits. At the same moment, Lucan's nose twitched.

Pete stood up. "We'll have to tell somebody! Call your aunt!"

"No." Jessie touched Lucan's hand and found it cool, not icy. A vein in the wrist throbbed against her fingertips. "Sh! Not so much noise. He's just asleep!"

"But," Pete began. Jessie cut him off.

"He's got a pulse. Feel it."

Pete touched Lucan's wrist. After a moment he nodded. But Jessie could see his face even in the dusk, and she knew that mulish expression.

"A minute ago he was like a piece of meat in the fridge. And he had no pulse. He was dead, Jess."

"Of course he wasn't dead. That's impossible!"

Lucan's eyes opened. No yawning and stretching for him. He was wide awake in the first instant. He looked at Jessie's face, then Pete's.

"I know: you saw me asleep. Now I suppose you have questions."

"Yeah. We have questions," Pete said. "You lied to us. You don't have porphyria. So what is wrong with you?"

Lucan studied his face. "Why don't you tell me?"

"A couple of minutes ago you were dead or next thing to it. I guess that's how you spend all your days."

"Only the really sunny ones."

Pete shook his head impatiently. "You hide from the sun. You live on blood. Then you run around all night." He took a breath. "Maybe you don't bite people on the neck, I don't know. But what about cows?"

"Why? Are you a vegetarian?"

"Answer the question!"

Lucan moved. One moment he was lying on the cot, the next he was kneeling on Pete's chest with his hands around Pete's throat, and cardboard cartons were bouncing everywhere.

Jessie dropped and grabbed at his hands. Lucan's eyes blazed at her. "Please," she said. "For me." His eyes dimmed. He shrugged slightly. Then he let go, stood up and backed away. Pete lurched to his feet, swatting dust off his clothes. He slid his hands into his back pockets (to hide their trembling, Jessie knew, because she knew Pete) and squared his shoulders.

"So? What kind of a monster are you?" Same old Pete, wouldn't back down an inch.

Lucan didn't answer. He stood so still, eyes unfocused, that Jessie began to think he had forgotten they were there.

Then his eyes woke up and sparkled. He winked at her, tapped a forefinger on his lips and cat-footed across the floorboards to the top of the iron staircase. Not a creak sounded under his feet. He smiled at Jessie and made the shushing sign again.

Then, so suddenly that she gasped, he dropped into the stairwell. There was a squeal, some clanging, muffled cries, and Lucan climbed the stairs again. His arms were full of something that struggled. Long red hair flailed upside-down.

Jessie jumped forward. "Oh, no!"

IT TOOK ABOUT five minutes for Jessie to convince Lucan it was safe to unpin Marianne's arms and take his hand off her mouth. They had to make Marianne nod Yes to a promise not to scream.

"And don't just run away," Jessie said, "not 'til you know what's what. Okay?" Marianne nodded again. "Okay," Jessie said.

Lucan let her go. She stumbled away, whirled around, and stabbed a finger at him. "I was right! Jessie's been hiding somebody, and it's you!"

"Smart!" Lucan smiled at her. "What else do you know?"

"You're the reason Dr. Erasmus was here yesterday!" Marianne stuck close to the stair head, poised to escape. Scared, but she hadn't panicked, Jessie saw. *Not a wimp, our Marianne.*

"How much did you hear?" Jessie asked.

"Everything. Right from Pete saying *that one* was dead. What is he?"

Lucan sat down on the cot. He tilted his head. "What do you think?"

Marianne tossed back her hair and flipped a hand, trying hard to look as if she met people like Lucan every day. "You're one of the u-undead, right?"

He sniffed a laugh. "You mean I turn myself into a bat and fly around biting people on the neck?"

"Well, no, I was thinking more like Angel in *Buffy*. Or that studly Edward Cullen."

"Marianne! This is not a movie!" Jessie pointed. "This is Lucan. He's Dr. Erasmus's son, and he ran away because he's been abused, and he's staying here another couple of days. That's all there is to it."

"It didn't sound like all."

"It's not all," Pete said.

"Okay. Let's see, where do I start?" Lucan bent, felt under the cot for a bottle of water, and chugged it. He wiped water from his chin. He looked completely... Not ordinary, Jessie didn't think he ever could look ordinary. But normal. Some of the tension seeped out of the attic.

"You could start with what Marianne said." Jessie sat down on the cot beside him.

"Right, undead. Well, I'm not one of the undead, Marianne, because I was never dead. Do I drink blood? Yes, and I've explained that. It's about all I can digest. Oh, and water." He waggled the bottle. "But if you turn on that light you'll see I cast a shadow. And you can see me in a mirror, right, Jessie?"

She thought back. "Uh-huh."

"And I can try until I turn blue, but I'll never turn into a mist and float out the window." He turned up his free hand, *what the heck*. "Now, Pete. Why do I sleep all day? Because the sun makes me tired, even when it's hidden, you know that." He looked at Marianne. "It's a genetic thing." Back to Pete. "And why was I cold? My metabolism (that means my *energy*, Pete) is really low when I sleep. Now I'm warm. Have I left out anything?"

Pete said, slow and deliberate: "You. Had. No. Pulse."

"I had a very weak pulse."

"No. None."

"Have it your own way." Lucan capped the water bottle and dropped it on the cot. "Bring me some garlic. It'll make me sick because I can't digest it, but it won't send me into fits. What else can I tell you?"

"That cage you were in," Jessie said suddenly, surprising herself. She didn't want to quiz him. But the question shouldered to the front of her mind and jumped out. "It was made of silver, wasn't it?"

"Yes." He looked at her distantly.

"Why?"

84

"Another allergy. I can't touch the stuff. That was one of my father's bright ideas, of course. He wanted to be sure I had no chance to escape. He'd been planning this thing for a long time."

It was true, but it wasn't the whole truth. She knew it but didn't challenge him. Pete looked baffled but no longer horrified. Marianne had inched forward until she was standing behind Pete.

"Still think I'm some kind of monster?" Lucan looked at Marianne and bent up one side of his mouth. She shook her head.

"Good." He looked from face to face. "Because I need your help."

"Again?" Pete's dark eyebrows rose.

"I mean I really need help. Like I told Jessie yesterday."

"Help with your father." She took a deep breath. "Okay, you've got mine, anyway. But what exactly can we do?"

"Give me some of your blood."

It almost emptied the attic.

Jessie wondered why she wasn't outraged, the way Pete was, or hysterical, the way Marianne was. As the night deepened she felt herself growing more alert, full of energy, ready to handle anything. Even Lucan couldn't scare her. Much.

"Look," he said. "It wouldn't be a lot of blood. Just a few drops from each of you. It'll mean the difference between life and death to me." Maybe it was the honest desperation in his voice that kept the other two from crashing down the stairs.

"And I could make it worth your while," he added. Jessie's head went up. Something new was in his voice. It was velvety, hard to resist, a dark chocolate kind of voice. "There are things I can do. Strings I can pull."

"Like what?" Marianne asked.

Pete hunched his shoulders. "Later. Let's get out of here. This attic gives me the creeps."

Jessie shook her head. "You go. We can't. Aunt Steffie's home for dinner."

"Actually, she's not." Marianne poked a hand into her back pocket. "You know, I didn't come here to lurk. I was looking for you," she looked at Jessie, "to give you this." She tossed over a bit of folded money. Jessie caught it. "Didn't find you in your room, so I thought I'd try your secret hideaway, and bingo!"

Jessie unfolded the bill. "Ten dollars?"

"Yeah. Mom's gone out to supper with a girlfriend. That's why she came home early. Not to bond with her daughter, oh no." She rolled her eyes skyward.

"But what about your spaghetti?"

"The sauce will keep in the fridge 'til the weekend, Mom says. The money's for take-out. I got the same."

"That's cool." Pete bounced up. "We'll all eat out. I'll phone my mom."

"But Lucan can't!" Jessie said. "It's too dangerous! His father's men might see him."

Lucan stood up and stretched his fists to the rafters. "Don't worry, Jessie. He won't just grab me off the street. It's not his way to do things out in the open like that. And when we meet…" He smiled, and it was the smile Jessie didn't like. "It'll be because I'm ready. He won't have things all his own way."

Chapter 17

The Smell of Fear

IT WAS STILL not much past seven-thirty. Cars and trucks bumped and beeped along King Street, parents herded children into the supermarket, two men carried a ladder out of the hardware store.

Jessie expected Marianne to split off and find some of her friends to hang with. Instead she stuck with her and Pete and Lucan. In two minutes Jessie had it figured out. Lucan was the big draw. Marianne was fascinated, and she didn't hide it. She kept tossing back her red mane and trying to catch his eyes. Typical Marianne, Jessie thought.

But while Pete and Marianne bought cheeseburgers and doughnuts from a shop that blazed with light-reflecting chrome, Lucan waited outside with Jessie. Lucan said the burgers would be nowhere near rare enough for him, and Jessie was too keyed up to eat anything.

And too distracted. From the moment they left the house, she'd been getting random whiffs of odours. As she stood outside the burger place, the smell of raw beef slid out of the kitchen and past all the cooking smells, and slapped her in the nose. Then that vanished and a moment later her sinuses were stinging with the aroma of vinegar.

Something's happened to my sense of smell. Am I sick? Or is it all in my head?

"So where're you going to live?" Marianne asked as they crossed the King Street bridge. "I mean, after you move out of our attic? Not that I'm pushing."

"His mother's parents," Jessie put in.

"That's a crock," Pete said, between bites of doughnut.

Lucan shrugged both shoulders high. "All right, I lied about that. There were no grandparents. No relatives at all. I was raised in the country and I never went to school. There was a nanny and later there was a tutor. I hardly ever saw a regular person."

He lied. Jessie tried not to feel bad about that. He'd needed time to trust them, just at first, that was all. Maybe he'd never learned to trust, because nobody had ever cared about him.

"So where will you live?" Marianne persisted.

"Oh, I'll work something out." Lucan flipped a careless hand. "Don't you worry about me."

He strolled across the street and a truck swerved to miss him. The other three waited for traffic to pass, then ran across the street after him. They turned onto Iroquois Road, away from Finnismore's tiny downtown.

"Sounds like there was money to burn, where you grew up," Marianne said.

"Sure! I had a swimming pool all to myself and a wall-sized TV and the top-of-the-line ATV and my own games room. But no father, no mother," he added flatly. "No friends."

"Was all the rest lies, too?" Pete asked. "All that about him wanting to kill you?"

"Oh, no. That's all true. That's why I need your blood."

A leather-faced farmer in a feed mill cap gave them a shocked look and walked past them shaking his head.

"Not good enough," Pete said.

"Okay, look. This is how it is. I'll have to have it out with my father. But right this minute, he's much stronger than I am. I'd have no chance." He put up his chin and walked faster, as if to outdistance any more questions.

At Jasper Street they left the pavement and crossed the park to the baseball diamond. Just one game was set for today, and it was already over. The last cars and pickup trucks were turning out of the parking lot. The field lights were still on, and the concession booth was lit up, but nobody was in the booth. The only people in sight were two parks department workers picking up trash on the far side of the field.

The empty bleachers gleamed under the dazzling lights like ribs picked clean by vultures. Lucan took a run and went leaping from seat to seat up to the top.

Jessie sprang after him. Tension snapped like popcorn inside her. It felt delicious to move. Reaching the top row she spread her arms wide. One more leap and she'd swoop right off the back of the bleachers and into the sky!

"Whoops!" Lucan caught her arm and swung her around onto a seat. "Not yet," he whispered.

She laughed. "What does that mean?"

Lucan shook his head. "Later." By then the other two had climbed to join them. They sat in a row along the top tier: Lucan at one end, Jessie beside him, then Pete, then Marianne.

Pete scowled up at the nearly-full moon. "I still don't get it. What d'you mean, stronger? You and your dad planning to arm-wrestle?"

"I think Jessie will understand," Lucan answered in the measured way that made him seem so much older than Pete. "I'm talking about the kind of strength that comes from inside. It's part energy, and part will power. It's the kind of strength that needs blood to grow."

"Crap!"

"Blood is strength," Lucan said. "Blood is life." There was something in his quiet voice that silenced them all, even Pete.

Then a new odour stung Jessie's nose. "Wuh!" She sniffed, but the chill air only smelled of cut grass and composting leaves and wooden planks that had been warming in the sun all day.

"What's that?"

"Sh." Lucan's warm fingers wrapped around hers. "Use your mind. Not your nose."

Use my mind? A beat, and then she knew what he meant. She remembered the sour green fog of dislike, or was it jealousy? that she'd seen and smelled around Pete, and the red prickle of anger on Marianne's face.

This was like that, but different. It smelled like rotten eggs and roses, putrid and sweet at the same time. Fear mixed with fascination. *What is this?*

Somehow she knew it wasn't coming from Pete or Marianne. Not Lucan, for sure: he smelled like... like... *cat, ginger, ammonia, cold earth, hot blood, steel, bone...*

He pressed her wrist. *Focus, Jessie.* Had he said that aloud or not?

Not. What do you smell?

Someone's near. Someone I don't know. She looked around. Whoever it was, they had to be almost within arm's reach: the sweet, sick smell in her head was that strong. But where? From their seat in the top row of the bleachers, there was nothing to see but the empty ballpark.

Lucan turned his head, met her eyes and winked. Then he put a hand on the railing behind him and with a twist of his body, without a sound, flipped up and over and was gone.

Jessie gasped. Pete and Marianne swivelled around. Lucan had dropped into the darkness behind the bleachers so silently and so fast, you'd think he'd evaporated.

There was a yelp from the seats underneath them, then scuffling sounds, and a big figure blundered out into the light with Lucan behind him, pinning his arms.

Chapter 18

A Dark Radiance

JESSIE ALMOST laughed. She'd been expecting one of Dr. Erasmus's hounds, or more than one. But Kenny?

He lurched back and forth, trying to break free, but Lucan's thin hands gripped him like steel handcuffs. By this time the other three had climbed down and run around to the back of the bleachers. Jessie goggled. Kenny looked nearly twice Lucan's size.

Marianne hovered at Lucan's elbow. "Let him go! He'll get us in trouble!"

"Not now, he won't." Lucan suddenly released him. Kenny staggered a few steps, then lurched around to face him, breathing hard.

"I wasn't spying!"

"You were hiding and listening. What else would you call it?" Lucan walked slowly toward him.

Kenny backed away. "I was stacking the empty cartons, there, for recycling." He pointed backward, not taking his eyes off Lucan. "I didn't mean to listen! I swear!"

"Lucan." Jessie put a hand on his arm. Then pulled it away. Something electric and jagged was jumping off his skin. "Lucan, he's no harm to us! Let it go!"

Kenny's eyes were so wide you could see the whites all around them. The sour fear smell rolled off him in waves.

"You know who I am, Kenny?" Lucan took another slow step.

"You're Dr. Erasmus's kid."

"What else am I, Kenny?"

Pete moved as if to step between them, but stopped before he got that far. "Lucan, he's had enough! Leave him alone!"

Kenny stopped backing away. "Blood. You said ... blood."

"So what, Kenny?"

"That was you at that farm, wasn't it?"

"What farm, Kenny?"

Jessie couldn't see Lucan's face, but Kenny let out a cry.

She grabbed Lucan's arm and this time held on. Her hands tingled. "What are you doing?"

"Nothing yet." He kept his eyes on Kenny, hard and sharp as two knives. "He has to be shut up."

"But you can't just... " She thought of the hired man's crushed limbs. Lucan turned his head. His eyes smiled at her and she knew he might as well have been inside her skull.

"I have to do something about him, Jessie. He'll make my life impossible if I don't. Yours, too. Step away, Pete."

Pete had gone over to Kenny and was talking to him. "Just go. Never mind him." He ignored Lucan. Kenny ignored Pete and watched Lucan with his white-rimmed eyes.

"Lucan, you'll make things worse." Jessie shook his arm. "Stop it!"

"Well, maybe there's another way." He looked at Kenny again. "You. Are you listening?"

Kenny nodded and swallowed.

"You never saw me. Understand? You never heard what we said." Lucan's voice wove tendrils through Jessie's mind. She saw a dark radiance all around him, like the glow of sunlight in a negative photo: brightness turned inside out. She let go of his arm and backed away.

"Never saw you," Kenny said dully. "Never heard you."

"You don't know me," Lucan said, downy-soft, irresistible.

"Right?"

"Don't know you."

"Go."

Kenny rubbed his eyes, looked around vaguely as if he wasn't sure how he'd got there, then turned and trudged away across the park.

The field lights went off. Moonlight though the slats of the bleachers striped their faces black and silver. Lucan tossed back his moon-white hair. "There. Good as new. And no longer a problem." The dark radiance around him was gone.

"What did you do to him?" Pete's voice shook. "What was that, some kind of hypnotism?"

"No! Will-power, that's all. Or charisma, that would cover it. I just made him see things my way."

There was more to it than that, a lot more, but Jessie couldn't find the right words.

Marianne's fingernails dug into her bicep. A stream of emotions tumbled through her hand and up Jessie's arm. Fear, astonishment, admiration. Jessie blinked at her. Admiration?

"What was that you did just then?" Marianne demanded. "Could you do it again? For me?"

"For you!" Lucan's eyebrows flickered. "Well, that depends." He stepped out from under the bleachers. "Remember what I said? I need help. Fair exchange. How about it, Pete?"

"Drink my blood? You're crazy." Pete grabbed Jessie's hand. "Come on, let's go. Any second now he'll be zapping our brains, like he did to Kenny."

"I would never force you. I wouldn't do that to a friend."

"Friend!" Pete snorted. But Jessie knew the words were for her.

She ignored Pete's pull on her hand. The real pressure was inside. When Lucan said he needed her, he was telling the truth. She knew that for sure. And last night he'd saved her life.

"Am I asking too much?" he said quietly.

"I… I don't know."

"Even though our blood's already mixed? How could losing a little more hurt you?"

Her right palm stung, as if he'd poked it with a stick. She'd almost forgotten what happened, the night they'd helped him escape. Their hands clasped and bleeding together.

She wet her lips. "I don't know what you want. I don't know what you are. I'm afraid."

"Never be afraid of me, Jessie," he said, too soft for the others to hear. "I'd never hurt you. Never."

She wavered. Then remembered Kenny's empty eyes. He'd been drained of something, as sure as if he'd lost blood.

"Please?" Softer still.

"I can't. Not any more."

"I thought we were friends. You promised you'd help."

"We are friends! But this… I can't."

"You promised!"

It hurt to say no. She couldn't get the word out, just kept shaking her head. Lucan stood statue-still, eyes dark holes in a silver mask.

Pete got a firm grip on her wrist. "C'mon. This could get bad." He started away, pulling her with him. "Marianne, come on!"

"Wait!" Marianne ran to Lucan. Their heads bent together and they whispered. A moment later she backed away. "Bargain?" she called, still walking backwards.

"Bargain!" Lucan laughed and slipped into the striped darkness under the bleachers.

Marianne turned and ran past Jessie and Pete. Her face was sharp with fear and excitement.

"Marianne!" Jessie called. "What did you do? What happened?"

"Maybe nothing," Marianne shouted back as she ran. "Maybe the best thing ever!"

Jessie clutched at her hair. Danger was in the air, things were moving too fast. She looked back at the bleachers, but there was no sign of Lucan.

Then she looked again. Someone was out in the middle of the diamond, on the pitcher's mound. Not Lucan, not Dr. Erasmus, not one of the hounds. Somebody familiar.

He stood quietly, watching. Grey, calm, featureless as a shadow or a stone. Jessie was sure he'd heard every word, seen every change of expression.

"Pete." She felt backwards for his arm. "Look there. The grey man. There he is again!"

"Who? Where?"

She glanced impatiently at Pete, then waved at the pitcher's mound. "There!" But when she turned her head again, nobody was there. The diamond lay empty in the moonlight.

Chapter 19

Running Down the Moon

"HE BETTER NOT show up in your attic again," Pete said. They'd stopped at the corner of King and Mercy, the place where they usually split up, Pete going one way home and Jessie the other.

"After all that?" she said. "He won't. He'll find somewhere else."

"'Cause what he did to Kenny, that was bad."

"I know."

"He's dangerous, Jess. I don't know how he did that, but he's screwed up."

"Gotta go. Curfew." She started along Mercy Street.

"Jessie!" Pete called after her.

"Yeah?"

"If he shows up, what'll you do?"

She stood still and thought about it.

"You'll tell him to bugger off, right?"

"Right," she said, although she wasn't all that sure. *I promised to help him. I did promise.* Why was it so hard to get past that?

"MARIANNE?" Jessie banged on Marianne's bedroom door. "Open up!"

"Get lost!" Marianne shouted from the other side. "I'm on the phone!"

"What's this bargain you made with Lucan?"

"None of your beeswax!"

"Marianne, you've got to tell me!"

No answer, only a blast of music from behind the door. That was sort of an answer, Jessie supposed.

It was still barely nine o'clock. Homework, Jessie thought. She had at least three assignments due tomorrow, or overdue. She never missed school deadlines. Never, that is, until Lucan slipped out of that silver cage and into her life.

Well, Lucan was gone now. Maybe forever. That would be best.

She shut herself into her room and spent the next hour reading a chapter of *The Outsiders* for English. At the end of the hour she realized she'd been reading the same page over and over again. She threw the book into a corner.

Then went and picked it up and stacked it neatly on her desk with the others. She never used to throw books, either.

Ten o'clock. She washed, brushed her teeth, and changed into pyjamas. Not satin ones like Marianne's, which she'd always thought silly, because satin stuck to you in bed and got all creased. Jessie's pyjamas were long-sleeved white cotton flannelette printed with a design of stars and crescent moons. The moons made her think of Lucan, and the moondial in his father's garden.

She got into bed, lay in the dark a while staring at the ceiling, then got out of bed again. No use trying to sleep. Her eyelids felt wired open. Her feet were pins and needles, they had to move. She paced around the room in the dark, not needing any more light than what came under her door from the hall.

She suddenly thought of circling the room walking just on the tops of things, like a cat: dresser, desk, bed, window sills, doorknobs. Why not? She tried it, made it halfway around, to the knob of the closet door, teetered there on one foot, and dropped to the floor with a thump.

She sat on the bed and giggled at herself. "I'm going crazy. Lucan's made me crazy."

Eleven o'clock. The light under her door went out. The music from Marianne's room went silent, finally! Jessie listened for creaks overhead, the sound of someone walking across the attic floor, but it never came.

He won't be back. Good thing, too. Pete's right, he's dangerous.

She stood at the window looking down. No sign of him out there, no stealthy shadows. The moon was high. It filled the back yard and the lane with light like clear water. She opened her window and slid the screen up. Reached out a hand to see it turn bright. The cut on her palm was all healed up, almost invisible. She cupped her hand and imagined drinking the silver light from her palm. She tried it. Almost tasted…

"Dangerous," she said, giggling again. "He made me cuckoo! And now Marianne's agreed on who-knows-what with him." Her smile faded. "Something's going to happen. Something bad. I have to find out what's going on!"

Lucan! Where are you, what are you up to?

She wasn't expecting an answer, but suddenly his laughter filled her mind. It sounded/felt as if he was near, within arm's reach.

Not that close. But close.

She stood back from the window. "He's in the house!"

No. But near.

"How are you doing this? How are you in my mind?"

We're blood siblings, remember? We're linked.

"Tell me what's going on!"

Come find me! And maybe I'll tell.

His laughter faded.

"Wait!" Jessie leaped at the window and was halfway through it before she realized what she was doing. *I'm no wall-climber.* She squirmed back inside, closed the window and ran on tiptoe downstairs to the kitchen.

98

Breaking curfew again. *I'm turning into a real delinquent.* She unlocked the door and stepped outside. The wind slipped cold fingers down her neck and her feet slid on the damp grass. She realized then that she was wearing just her pyjamas, and her feet were bare, and the night was cold. That bothered her only distantly. More worrisome was the thought: *If I'm caught this'll mean big trouble.*

She mused on that a moment, looked back at the house, then shook her head. *Bigger trouble if I don't find Lucan.* Distant laughter lilted through her head. She closed her eyes and focused. North. Once out the gate, she began to run.

SOMETIME during the night Jessie forgot why she was tracking Lucan. She was trapped in a spell of moonlight and motion, the rhythmic slap of her feet on pavement, their soft thud on grass.

She never grew tired. The moon sailed down the sky, and Jessie ran. Voices shouted. She left them far behind. The night smelled of frost, the grass sparkled like diamonds. She was never cold, her blood ran too hot for that.

She ran and ran and ran. Until, in the space of ten footfalls, the magic drained away. She thudded to a stop and stood swaying. Then her knees gave way and she sat down on somebody's lawn. Icy wetness seeped through the seat of her pyjamas.

Her heart slowed, her breath slowed. She looked up and the moon was gone. The sky in the east glowed violet behind the trees. It was nearly dawn.

"I've been out all night!"

Not quite.

"Where am I?"

Look around.

She looked around. The trees and houses looked familiar. This was Mercy Street. She was sitting on her own lawn in pyjamas and bare feet, shuddering with cold. Her feet were bleeding and black with grime.

"You've been playing games with me, right? This is your idea of fun."

Hide and seek! He laughed.

"No fair, I'm always It. You never let me catch you."

"Well, the game's over now."

She looked over her shoulder. Lucan was sitting on the front steps. He touched the step beside him. "Home free!"

"We have to talk." She struggled to her feet and took a step, wincing. "About Marianne."

"That's between me and Marianne. You'd better get to bed before they discover you're out. Wash your feet first." He smiled his secretive smile. "You're not really up to this. Not yet."

Before she could ask him what that meant, he stood up and stepped past her and jogged away down the street. She limped to the sidewalk, calling, but he was gone so quick, you'd think the shadows between the streetlights had soaked him up.

Chapter 20

Clues and Treasures

AGAIN THE FIGURE darting across the road, the swerve, the scream, the blackness, the face at the jagged window. Only, this time, the screaming went on and on and on.

Make it stop!

Jessie clawed her way out of the dream and lay gasping. The screaming had stopped but the air still vibrated. She wondered if she'd been the one making that horrible noise.

The room was dim, but not dark. The glowing blue numbers on the digital clock said 11:45. It was a long minute before she remembered that was a.m., not p.m. She'd been dozing all morning with the curtains closed tight.

Friday, she thought dully. Should be at school.

Then: *Friday! Lucan's birthday!*

She levered herself up until she was sitting on the edge of the bed, where she huddled, shivering, wrapped in the coverlet. She was still wearing last night's pyjamas; the backside and pant cuffs felt stiff and gritty. Her brain felt stuffed with feathers.

"Food," she muttered. It struck her that she hadn't had a thing to eat since yesterday's tiny bite of tuna sandwich. That was probably why she felt so woozy.

Once the thought was in her head, hunger bit. She felt hollowed out. She lurched off the bed, dragging the coverlet after her like a long shawl, and shuffled out into the hall on bruised and swollen feet. The brightness from the end window made her eyes water. She squeezed them nearly shut and groped toward the stairs, one hand on the wall, guiding herself by flickering glances through her eyelashes.

Passing the mirror, she caught a glimpse of a white-faced creature with purple shadows under its eyes and hair sticking up in all directions. Then the screaming started again.

She recognized it now. Telephone. The sound sent needles through her eardrums. She stumbled and slid down the stairs to the alcove behind the kitchen door and grabbed up the receiver on the fourth ring.

"Jess! You okay?" Pete's voice blasted from the receiver.

Jessie held it away from her ear. "Ow! Don't yell!"

"Are you still sick? Why aren't you at school?"

"Sick, no. I don't know. Just really tired. I stayed up last night."

"Why?" Something in Pete's voice changed. "Don't tell me. Lucan."

"I had to talk to him."

"I thought you were going to stay away from him."

"I had to ask him about this bargain, whatever it is, he's fixing up with Marianne. I tried." She rubbed the aching hollow next to her right eye. "Didn't get anything out of him."

"I saw Marianne sailing around school today. She looked as if she was next up for *Canada's Got Talent*. You know: scared, excited. I couldn't get her to stop moving long enough to talk."

"I wish I knew what she asked him." Jessie slid down the wall to sit on the floor. "I sort of remember … sometime last night … something Lucan did, somewhere he went … a clue."

"I can hardly hear you. How sick are you? Want me to come over?"

"No. I'll eat. I'll sleep. I'll be fine. See you later."

For a long time Jessie sat on the floor in the dim alcove, looking at her bare feet, which were clean (although she couldn't recall wash-

102

ing them), and thinking of all the ways Lucan and his father were different from ordinary people. No matter how she tried to fit the pieces together, she had a feeling that some bits were missing. She couldn't make out the whole picture.

She wondered where Lucan was now, and what he was doing.

Lucan? This is your big day! Where are you?

A smell seeped through her brain. Damp concrete, a trace of engine oil, a whiff of mildewed wood. Her mind flooded with darkness without a ray of light.

It was like being buried alive. The scent-image was unbearable. She staggered to her feet, shedding the coverlet, and groped into the kitchen, where a cruel blaze of sunshine nearly drove her out again. Shielding her eyes with one arm, she darted at the window and yanked at the cord of the blinds. They rattled down and brought back a comforting dusk.

She opened the refrigerator. Milk, cheese, yogurt, potato salad. She set her teeth against a wave of nausea and shut the fridge. The cupboards offered Rice Krispies, canned mushroom soup, wheat crackers and orange pekoe tea. *I should be able to swallow tea, at least.*

She reached up for the canister. Behind it, in a back corner where she'd never looked before, was a small, brown cardboard box with "Jessie" printed on it in Steffie's neat, rounded hand. Ten seconds later Jessie had the box open on the kitchen table.

There wasn't much in it. Just a black leather wallet, a little zippered green brocade case, and some old photos of herself and her parents. Her eyes stung. Why hadn't Steffie given her these things? Too busy? Just forgot?

No. Because it would have hurt too much and she knew it.

Hunger forgotten, Jessie sat down at the table to inspect her inheritance. The little brocade case held her mother's good jewellery. A

103

gold chain with a pearl drop, a pair of gold hoop earrings, a twisted silver bangle, a gold ring set with jade.

She slipped the bangle over her wrist and then, with a shiver of distaste, dropped it back into the case. Something twigged in her mind, but another part of her mind knew the thought was unwelcome and kicked it out.

She spread out the photos and studied the faces. All the scenes were sunny, all the people looked happy. And all were gone now, even the girl who sat with her father's arm around her. Gone away into a world of warmth and love and colour where Jessie couldn't follow.

She thought her heart would tear loose from her body.

Steffie was right not to give me these.

Jessie shuffled the photos together. She left on top the one of her father and herself, taken just over a year ago, not long before the car accident. In that one her father wasn't looking at the daughter under his arm. He was looking straight out at Jessie.

At the camera, she corrected herself. But she couldn't erase the feeling that he was looking right at her, trying to tell her something with those serious brown eyes. *Jessie. Take care.*

The last thing in the box was her father's wallet. It was old and worn, the soft leather still pressed into a curve from the back pocket where he'd always carried it. Jessie bit her lip, straightened her shoulders and then swiftly emptied it.

Not many surprises. More photos, including a copy of the one with herself under his arm. Couple of credit cards, his social insurance card, a few business cards, a twenty-dollar bill.

And a cheque for $220 made out to Clement Brown and signed by August Erasmus. Jessie frowned at the tall, sharp signature. Payment for the work her father had done at the Erasmus house. She turned the slip of paper over. There was no bank stamp on the back.

104

He'd never cashed the cheque. Why not?

And here was another funny thing. She picked up one of the business cards. *Eugenia Palmer, Psychic*, it announced in flowing silver letters on a sky-blue background. Underneath it said: *Horo-scopes   Herbal Remedies   Dream Work.*

Jessie shook her head over the card. What could it be doing in Dad's wallet? He'd always laughed at astrology and Ouija boards and ghost stories and such stuff.

The card smelled funny, too. Jessie sniffed it, then wrinkled her nose. She turned it over and found a scrap of some herb flattened under a strip of transparent tape. The tiny bit of leaf had a stink out of all proportion to its size. She pulled it off and carried it to the trash can under the sink, then washed her hands.

She climbed the stairs to her room, taking the box and the coverlet with her. The box went into her top dresser drawer. But first she took out the photo of her father and herself and stuck it under the frame of the mirror. As she moved across the room toward the bed, his eyes seemed to follow her. *Take care, Jessie. Take care.*

Chapter 21

Jessie Blooms

THE DREAM AGAIN. This time it was different. An ounce of courage had come to her from somewhere. This time she dared to look longer, to see more.

Only a dream, she told herself, even as she dreamed. Not really happening.

That figure dashing across the road, a split-second glimpse in the reeling headlights. Something familiar as the head turned.

Then darkness. And then the jagged window shape suddenly filled with the face looking in. The slow smile. A bland, grey face, with eyes that looked at her from a million miles away.

No!

But this time, when Jessie woke, the scene was solid in her memory. And she knew one thing. The first time, it hadn't been a dream.

"It really happened. That's the way it was," Jessie said aloud. "He was there, at the accident, that man. Dr. Erasmus's driver." Or caretaker, or whatever he was. The grey man. Maybe he'd even caused the accident by jumping in front of the car. On purpose?

And ever since she'd freed Lucan, the grey man had been watching her.

She sat up and hugged her knees. There were a lot of links between her father and Dr. Erasmus, now that she thought about it. Dad's work on the silver lock, the uncashed cheque, the grey man at the accident. And the way Erasmus had talked about Dad, called him a busybody.

The light leaking around the curtains was cool and blue now, easy on the eyes. The clock by the bed said 7:05. Jessie stretched out her arms and legs and felt energy bubble back in like warm ginger ale. *Yes! Getting better!* Even her feet felt less sore.

As she slid out of bed, a door closed below and a moment later quick steps ran up the stairs. A tap on her door, and Steffie looked in. She smiled.

"So you're up! Feeling more like yourself?"

"You bet! Guess I just needed that sleep. I'll get washed and dressed now." She made a face at her pyjamas and hoped Steffie wouldn't notice, in the dimness, how dirty they were.

"I brought home two nice little steaks for you and Marianne. But if you're not up to that, I'll leave some soup on the stove for you."

"Aren't you eating with us?"

"No, I'm ... I'm meeting someone. A friend." Steffie's eyes were bright. In fact, she looked bright all over, happier than Jessie had seen her look for months. Who was this friend?

"So, what'll it be?" Steffie asked. "Soup or steak?"

"Steak, please," Jessie said quickly. "And let me cook: I like mine rare."

After the door closed she stood and listened to what she'd just said.

Rare? I've never liked rare meat.

Blood sizzled in her veins. Energy prickled at her fingertips. And deep under her skin, in the marrow of her bones, hunger gnawed.

Jessie walked slowly across the room to the dresser. She looked into the mirror and saw a stranger. Herself, yet not herself. Not the sick, wan, bedraggled creature of this morning.

"I look... almost... "

Almost beautiful.

107

"But that's crazy!" She'd always thought of herself as just ordinary, not pretty, not ugly. But now?

Dark hair swinging like silk around a radiantly pale face. Eyes an amber glow, lips blooming with life.

The way Lucan comes alive at sunset. The way he glows by night.

She felt her forehead. Hot and dry, like Lucan's fingers. "I have a fever," she said to her father's photo. "That's where my colour comes from. Two or three days, and I'll be my plain old self again. You'll see."

Clement's eyes looked back at her sadly.

Chapter 22

Marianne's Bargain

"THAT'S REVOLTING." Marianne pointed a smeared finger at Jessie's plate. It was swimming with blood.

Jessie forked another piece of steak into her mouth and chewed. She didn't really want to swallow the meat, it felt heavy in her stomach. But the juices were delicious.

"You only grilled it for like two milliseconds!"

"It's healthier that way. Charring is bad for you, it causes cancer. Can't you sit down?"

Marianne wouldn't stop moving. Jesse had stopped trying to get information out of her. She had cut up her steak into small blackened pieces and was shimmying around the kitchen with her earbuds in, waving the plate and eating the bits with her fingers.

When her cell phone rang, she dropped the plate on the counter, tore off the earbuds and clapped the phone to her ear.

"Hi Mom! How's... oh! Really? Really? Yes!" She stared at Jessie, mouth open, eyes like lightbulbs. "Right! Later! Love ya!" Marianne flung the phone into the air and caught it and whooped. "He did it!"

Jessie pushed back her chair. "Who? What?"

"Lucan! He did it! My parents are getting back together!"

"Are you sure?"

"They're together right now. That was Mom. They're talking things out over dinner, she says. Oh, Jessie, I'm so happy!" Marianne grabbed Jessie and hugged her. Then pushed her off. "Sorry! I forgot you're not the huggy type."

"It's okay. I'm glad."

"You don't seem glad." Marianne headed for the door.

"I am. But wait!" She caught Marianne by the arm. "Wait just a minute. What's Lucan got to do with it?"

"He did it!" Marianne tried to pull free, but Jessie had found some extra strength along with the extra energy. She held on.

"You have to tell me. How do you know he did it?"

"Because he promised, yesterday. I saw how he'd persuaded Kenny, so I asked him to help."

"You asked him to do *that* to your parents?" Jessie's grip tightened. Memories from last night flew through her head. She'd sensed where Lucan had stopped longest. One place was in front of their house. Below Aunt Steffie's window. The other place...

"Wilton Street, near the river, isn't that where your dad lives now?"

"Yeah, but not for long. Ouch, let go, will you?"

"Lucan was watching him last night." She relaxed her grip.

"How would you know? Anyway, what's the big deal?" Marianne pulled free and headed along the hall toward the stairs. "No, he didn't zap their minds. He said he'd just sort of nudge them toward each other. It would only work if they really wanted it, and see, they do!" She stopped halfway up and added, "It's a talent he's got. A kind of charisma. Like he said."

It made sense, Jessie thought, as she ran up the stairs after Marianne. The Erasmuses would have needed a talent like this to survive. A gift for persuasion, maybe. Without it, their line probably would have ended a couple of centuries ago at the end of a sharpened stake.

Except it was more than persuasion. "There's something wrong about this. And what'll you have to do to pay for it?"

"Jessie, my parents are getting back together. Don't you think that's worth a little blood?"

"Blood!" Jessie grabbed Marianne's wrist and pulled her around. Marianne sat down with a thump on the top step.

"Yes, blood! And if you were any kind of a friend, you'd give him some of your blood, too."

"Aren't you the one who was gabbling on about the undead?"

Marianne waved that away with her free arm. "He's just sick. I should think you'd have a little more sympathy. Now will you stop grabbing me!"

"Will you stay still for half a second? Where're you going in such a big hurry, anyway?"

"To the attic."

"Why?"

"Lucan said to meet him there. He said, when I got the news, he'd meet me in the attic."

"I don't think you'd better."

"I have to!" Marianne kicked out and caught Jessie in the stomach. Jessie bent double. Marianne scrambled up and tore along the hallway to the closet door.

By the time Jessie got there, clutching her stomach, Marianne had the door open and the stairs unfolded. Jessie caught her on the second step. "Will you listen! I don't think he's sick. He's different. He's not like you and me."

Marianne was stubbornly shaking her head.

"I think he's not, well, not exactly human."

Marianne laughed. "Then what is he? An alien?"

"Maybe, in a way. No, listen! Maybe something changed in his family's genes, a long way back. And I don't mean porphyria."

"And that means he's bad, because he's different?"

"No, it means we don't know what he can do, or how he thinks. He could hurt you!"

"Let her go, Jessie." The voice floated down out of the dark. Without her willing it, her hand dropped. Marianne scampered up the stairs. Jessie followed cautiously, half expecting to be shoved back by an invisible hand.

Marianne was standing in the middle of the attic. Even in the dark Jessie could see her trembling.

"Over here," came the voice. Marianne walked across the attic to where Lucan stood beside the open window at the back. The opening was hardly big enough for a small child to crawl through. Yet Jessie was sure that was the way he'd come.

"Did I keep my side of the bargain?" he asked, soft and gentle, as if speaking to a small child.

"Y-yes," Marianne whispered.

"Let's go, then." He slipped an arm around her shoulders.

Jessie found her voice. "Marianne, you don't have to do it. You didn't know what you were promising."

"But if I back out?" She glanced up at Lucan's face.

"Then the deal's off." He was suddenly cool.

"And my mom and dad?"

He spread an open hand, as if letting something fall.

"Okay. I... I'll do it."

"Marianne, no!" Jessie started forward, or tried to. Her feet were stuck to the floor. Was Lucan doing that? He hadn't stopped her voice, though.

"Don't you remember what he said? A little blood from each of us. But without Pete and me, there's just you!"

Lucan's eyes flared at her through the dark. "Then it's your fault, Jessie. It's you that's putting Marianne in danger."

"So there is danger!"

He opened his mouth but didn't speak.

"Can't you see how wrong this is?"

112

"Wrong?" He sounded baffled.

"Of course, wrong. Taking blood from people. Not animals, people! To make yourself stronger."

"It's a transfusion. They do it all the time in hospitals." He was back in control, his eyes smiling.

"It's not a transfusion. It's just wrong."

He let go of Marianne and stepped closer to Jessie. Her feet were free now. She could have backed away, but she didn't.

"This is way past right and wrong, Jessie. This is life or death. My life, my death."

"It doesn't have to be. Don't go meet your father. Stay here!"

He looked at her as if she'd gone insane.

"Yes! You're sixteen now, he can't touch you. And we'll get Aunt Steffie to help. She'll do it when we explain how it's been for you. I know she will!"

He looked inward for a long moment. She held her breath. Then he tossed his head. "Won't work. I'd never be safe. He'll hunt me down, and he'll catch me when I'm not strong. No, it has to be now."

He walked back to the window and scooped Marianne under his arm. Her face was quiet, not like Marianne's face at all. Her stillness reminded Jessie of Kenny's empty eyes.

"So long, Jessie. You'll understand. Soon."

"Lucan, stop!"

She darted forward. But before she could reach them, Lucan slid first Marianne and then himself through the little window. He stretched and twisted and folded their two bodies like a pair of jellyfish. Jessie reached the window and looked out in time to see them, hand in hand, vault the back fence and vanish.

Chapter 23

Claws and Teeth

IT TOOK TWO phone calls to find Pete at school, where he was giving the Science Club mascots, two hamsters, their supper rations. After that it took five minutes for him to reach the baseball diamond. Jessie jogged and paced until Pete came pounding up the street.

Another ten minutes to reach the Erasmus house. It wouldn't have taken so long if Pete hadn't been so darn slow! Twice she had to stop and wait, dancing from foot to foot, until he caught up. She felt as if her blood was full of hot iron filings. Every time she looked at the moon, full now, and a little way up the eastern sky, she ached to race, to jump, to fly.

"What's the matter with you?" she snapped. "Any other time, you'd be way ahead of me!"

Pete shook his head, too winded to talk.

He got his breath back when they were crouching by the moondial, using the patch of asters as cover from the house. Nothing moved, no door slammed, no step sounded.

The windows were dark, except for the ones that took up most of the smaller third storey. That whole tier was a glowing box, filled with moonshine that slanted in from the east and out the other side.

"Looks like there's nobody home," Pete muttered.

"No: they're in there."

"But how can you be sure?"

"I just know." She couldn't explain it to herself, so how could she explain it to him? From the start there had been a thread tied between her and Lucan. Hour by hour, the thread had grown and thickened. Now all she had to do was think of him and she felt the tug. He was in there, and he wasn't alone.

A flicker, like sheet lightning, made her look up. But the sky was empty except for the sad-faced moon. Another flicker. She saw now that it came from the third storey. Someone in there was moving in and out of the shafts of moonlight, turning them on and off like winking eyes. "Somebody's up there."

"Let's go in, then." Pete sounded a lot more confident than he looked.

They found each other's hand and gripped tight, then let go. Jessie jumped up and raced to the house, Pete at her heels, and around to the back. At the back door, where they'd gone in on Tuesday, three days ago, to rescue an abused animal (only three days? It felt like three years!) they stopped.

Too much to expect the door to be unlocked this time, Jessie thought, and she was right. The handle didn't budge.

Pete pointed to the right. The window was a few feet away from the back door. It stood open an inch, the sash within reach of their hands. He ran to it, got his fingers under and strained, but nothing happened. "It's stuck."

"Hurry! Think of Marianne!"

"I am ... oof!"

"Here, let me help!" She squeezed in beside him and thrust her hands furiously at the sash. It held, then flew up with a screech. Something pattered on the floor inside.

She slid over the sill and Pete scrambled in after her. They stood in a kitchen. The white tile floor was littered with splinters of wood.

"That's the stick they used to keep the window from being forced up. What's left of it." Pete looked in wonder and a little fear at Jessie's hands.

"Must've been cracked. Come on!" She tiptoed across the room to the inner door. It opened onto a corridor that led forward to a high, wide hall. The floor here was a checkerboard of black and white and might have been marble.

Straight ahead was the front door. The way out. A little dim light came in through tall windows on either side. To the right a staircase swooped up to a shadowy landing, where it turned left and went up again. That way led to what Lucan had gone to face, the reason he'd needed their blood.

It suddenly hit Jessie. "This is stupid!" She thumped her forehead. "What got into me? Why didn't I call the police?"

"Because it would've taken hours to convince them," Pete whispered. "Not that we're doing a whole lot better. Wait a sec." He detoured to the front door and grasped the handle.

"We can't leave now!"

"Just making sure we can get out fast if we have to." He fumbled at the door and a lock clicked over, then another. "That could gain us a few seconds. We might need them."

"Smart!" Jessie grinned at him. He grinned back. Both grins were shaky, but better than wimpering in fear.

"Now…" Pete looked upward. He took a deep breath.

"Right." Jessie swallowed a lump of terror. She leaped for the stairs, her feet soundless on thick carpet.

She was one step below the landing when a movement up and to the left caught her eye. She grabbed the railing and swung herself to her knees on the step. Then peered around the bend on the stairs.

In the corridor above, a fold of cloth whisked out of sight. It might have been the hem of a coat: something shiny, like a wet raincoat.

Pete slid in beside her and touched her wrist: a question. She returned the touch, harder: *Wait*. They knelt listening, watching. Whis-

116

pers feathered the air, so faint they might have been the sound of the blood in her ears.

She thought of Lucan. A white radiance flooded her mind, and with it a terrible fear and fury, too near, too dangerous. She shut it out.

Can't do this. This is too much. She slid a foot backward.

Then she thought of Marianne, with her face emptied. She breathed deeply in and out several times and made her hands into fists to quiet their trembling. *All right. Ready or not, here we come.*

Silent on the carpet, she stood up and eased upward. Stepped out at last into the second-floor hall. Whirled to look all around. Moonlight flooded in through a tall window at the far end of the hallway. A matching window over the stairwell glowed dimly.

Enough light for Jessie's eyes. Nothing here but closed doors.

"What now?" Pete whispered. Then answered his own question by walking along the corridor, quietly opening and closing door after door. They all opened inward. Jessie followed him, sweating. He hadn't seen as much of Erasmus's hounds as she had. He didn't know enough to sweat.

"Ha," he breathed. The sixth door opened outward. On the other side were the bare wooden treads of a staircase. "Here we are!"

No warning. With a rush of air, they fell from the corridor ceiling like enormous bats. Their bodies glistened green-purple-black. Their eyes were yellow star-pricks in flat, scaly faces. Their wet jaws gaped wide.

Jessie tumbled into the doorway, knocking Pete off his feet. Two of the hounds landed in front of her and crouched to spring.

Along the corridor, other doors flew open and shiny bodies spilled out. They scuttled along the floor, they slithered up the walls and along the ceiling. The nearest hound spread claws, ready to leap.

Pete grabbed the door and pulled it shut. It wouldn't shut. A scaly

117

paw clutched the edge, digging trenches into the wood with its claws. Jessie kicked at the paw.

Pete hung onto the doorknob with both hands. Jessie clamped her hands over his and they strained back together. Right in front of their eyes gleamed a strong three-inch bolt. If they could ever get it closed!

The gap widened. The paw scrabbled, worked its way in. Now other claws hooked around the door at the top and bottom.

With a sudden heave, Pete threw all his weight backward. Outside the door came a chorus of whistling shrieks. Inside there was a crunch. The door crashed shut. Jessie whammed the bolt home.

Something flopped and scuffled at their feet. A bony ring closed on Jessie's ankle. Points of pain dug in. She screamed and kicked and kicked until it flew loose, then they both stamped and stamped. The scuffling sounds stopped.

Pete sank onto a step. Jessie oozed down beside him. They sat trembling together, shoulder to shoulder, listening to the scratching, gnawing sounds on the other side of the door.

It wasn't as dark as Jessie had thought at first. A faint light brushed down along the wall from above. She tilted back her head. The stairs went up to a landing, then turned and climbed in the other direction into a pale glow. The top of the stairwell must be open.

"I planned on creeping in without being noticed," she whispered.

"Not much chance of that now."

"They've gotta know we're coming."

"But nobody's stopped us. Why not?"

"Because they know they can stop us any time. We're no threat." Jessie listened to the frantic scratching on the other side of the door and rubbed her ankle. One thing was sure, there was no going back that way.

"Ready?" Pete nudged her with an elbow.

"I'll never be ready." She stood up. "Let's go."

Chapter 24
Blood on Marble

PETE LED THE WAY up the stairs, across the landing and up the final flight. They tried to step softly, but the wooden treads creaked under their weight. As Pete's head came level with the floor above, he stopped and pressed down on Jessie's shoulder.

Then he crept on hands and knees up the last few steps and slid around the banister post into a patch of white and black stripes: the shadow of the railing that protected the stairwell. It was the only cover there was. Jessie took one look at what was waiting above and slid after him.

If she'd had time to think about what she'd expected to see, it would have been some sort of Frankenstein's laboratory. Liquids bubbling through curly tubes, electrical gizmos crackling and sparking, a skull here and a stuffed crocodile there.

But there was nothing at all. The third storey was one big empty room, with windows on all four sides stretching to the ceiling. Skylights pierced the roof. Moonlight poured in from the east and out the west. It streamed across the floor, where metallic veins gleamed like lightning in the white marble tiles.

August Erasmus stood in the centre of the floor. Lucan faced him. August was wearing an ordinary dark business suit, white shirt and tie. But with the moonlight ghostly in his hair and the metallic veins forking under his feet, there was nothing ordinary about him. And everything alien about him was on the outside.

Lucan stood with his back to Pete and Jessie, still with Marianne

119

held close in the crook of his arm. Her head was on his shoulder. It looked like something out of a romantic movie, Jessie thought: young lovers facing up to the angry father.

Then Lucan turned his head to look down at the girl. A wet track glistened at the corner of his mouth. And Marianne...

Her head lolled back off his shoulder to show the ruin of her throat. Her hair was matted and dark. A sweet, strong smell made Jessie's head spin.

A part of her was crying silently for Dad. Another part, a stranger inside her body, yearned toward the sweet aroma. She found herself inching forward and froze, half in and half out of the patch of striped shadow.

Lucan pulled his arm from around Marianne and let her slide to the floor like an empty sack.

"We took too long," Pete groaned. "We came too late."

"Sh! No. Look."

The limp hand moved. Pete started forward. Jessie grabbed his arm. He turned on her. "She's alive! Now's our chance!"

"Not yet!"

Lucan was standing right over Marianne. Until he stepped away, there was no reaching her. Jessie thought forward at him and touched the edge of his tension: a steel spring compressed to its limit. She pulled her thought back.

"Yes, my son," Erasmus purred. "Oh, yes. Try. Kill me if you can." His eyes were bright slits. His lips peeled back over the long canine teeth.

Lucan smiled like a cat. A soft growl started deep in his throat. Then his smile sharpened and went wild and he lunged.

To Jessie it seemed that the two human figures were gone and two wild animals twisted in and out of the streams of moonlight. There was nothing human in their cries. She stared and trembled. Her

120

overloaded senses dragged her down like a lead overcoat.

Pete leaped up and sprinted to where Marianne lay. He skidded on the smeared marble and slithered the rest of the way on his hands and knees. Jessie gave herself a hard shake and followed. They each took an arm and started crawling back to the stairs, dragging Marianne between them.

The noise rose to a hellish pitch. Somebody was laughing like a maniac. Somebody was howling. Jessie thought she heard Lucan screaming her name. It nearly made her stop and go back.

Then, sudden as a thrown knife: silence. She did stop then, and huddled, and Pete with her. Marianne hadn't moved again.

The moonlight dimmed. Clouds, Jessie thought with the still sensible part of her mind. But to the rest of her it was as if everything around them was dying.

The moon came out again. One of the figures stood up with somebody's body drooping in his arms. His face tilted up to the moonlight. Eyes and teeth gleamed in a silent howl of triumph.

Gently, lovingly, August Erasmus laid Lucan's body down on the floor. He straightened up again and gazed down at his son's empty face. There were no marks on Lucan's face or throat. He could have been asleep, except he obviously wasn't. His eyes were open and as dead as two stones.

Lucan? Jessie reached for him with her mind. Nothing was there. Only a sense that someone had just gone, like the echo of a footstep in an empty room. *Oh, Lucan.*

Pete was tugging at her sleeve. When she looked at him he nudged her groggy face so she could see Erasmus, standing not two yards away, watching them with bright eyes.

"He'll kill us," she said. No need to whisper now.

"Back up. The stairs are right there."

"With those things at the bottom."

"We'll fight our way out. Better than waiting here."

But Erasmus didn't rush at them, he didn't pounce. Jessie saw that he wasn't looking at them at all. He was looking past them, at the stairwell. They might have been invisible.

At the bottom the door opened. *But we bolted it!*

Slow, quiet footsteps sounded on the stairs.

Chapter 25

A Basin of Moonlight

THE GREY MAN, the servant, came walking up the stairs. He carried a wide chrome basin that winked in the striped darkness. As he stepped into the flood of moonlight, the bowl filled. He held it out above Lucan's body. Light reflected upward into August Erasmus's face.

Erasmus dipped his hands into the basin of moonlight and began washing. He rubbed his eyes, passed his hands over his forehead and cheeks and throat. He dipped again and ran fingers over his head, smoothing his hair.

Jessie couldn't take her eyes off him. He was changing. As he washed and washed, the years sloughed away. Lines vanished from around eyes and mouth. Hollows filled. New, clear skin gleamed. The dead-white hair shone moon-silver.

The grey man stood holding out the basin, his quiet eyes on Erasmus's changing face. He hadn't even glanced at the three huddled by the stairwell.

Pete broke the spell first. He stood up. That woke Jessie. Together they dragged Marianne to the stairs and began the labour of carrying her down between them.

Nothing lay in wait for them at the bottom of the stairs. The door stood open. Nothing waited outside to drop on their heads. As they struggled along the corridor and down the swooping staircase to the ground floor, thumb-sized things scuttled along the baseboards and squirmed under rugs.

The front door opened at a touch and they were out, pulling in lungfuls of the clean, chill September air. Marianne was a dead weight between them as they staggered up the driveway toward the gate.

"The gate'll be locked," Jessie croaked. They'd climbed in over the wall. They would have to get Marianne out the same way. Which would be impossible.

A siren started wailing in the distance. Then another. Then nearer. It sounded like a pack of wolves racing in this direction.

"Somebody called for help," Pete said. "Who?"

An electric glare flooded the grounds, hiding the moon. Jessie squinted against the dazzle and saw the gates swing open, saw the grey man step aside. Ambulances and police cruisers poured howling around the gatepost and down the driveway. Caught in the glare, Jessie and Pete, with Marianne sagging between them, froze like deer.

"I DON'T THINK you really see what you've done." Sergeant Archer, Ontario Provincial Police, sounded calm, but Jessie could feel his anger, like blows of an invisible fist.

"Listen to him, Pete," Mr. Oliveiri said. He was baffled as well as angry. Pete had been in trouble before, but nothing like this.

Pete and Jessie sat side by side on two hard plastic chairs in the hospital waiting room. The grownups stood over them like judges looking down on a pair of disgusting criminals.

"All because you thought you had the right to take the law into your own hands," Archer went on from his enormous height, "an old man is dead. And your friend Marianne is next thing to it. Oh, and the dog's dead too. Satisfied?"

"Dog?" Pete gaped.

The sergeant thought he was clowning. He squatted down so he could glare up into Pete's face. "The dog you were going to rescue.

124

Remember? The dog you broke into private property to liberate. The dog that attacked Marianne when she opened its cage."

"Oh." Pete's face lit with understanding. It only made the sergeant angrier.

"The same damn dog Lucan Erasmus shot after his father pulled it off Marianne. You just count yourselves lucky he's not going to lay charges."

Jessie cleared her throat. "You … you said an old man died."

"Dr. Erasmus. Heart attack. Probably the stress of wrestling with the dog." Archer stood up with a grunt and turned away.

Out from under the spotlight for a moment, Jessie whispered: "He's thought of everything. A perfect story."

"But I didn't see that kind of a dog in that basement," Pete murmured back. "Not one big enough to do any damage, I mean."

"No, but you can bet he had one there for the police to see."

"A pit bull, probably."

"You know what bothers me?"

"The old man," Pete said.

"Yeah. It was Lucan who died, not Dr. Erasmus. Wasn't it?"

Aunt Steffie and Uncle Jason walked into the waiting room hand in hand, both of them pale and worn-looking but smiling. "She's going to be all right!" Uncle Jason said. "It isn't as bad as it looked, and she's already started healing, the doctor says. They're giving her plasma to replace the blood she lost."

Jessie's heart lightened to see them holding hands. So Marianne would have her wish. She hadn't lost all that blood for nothing.

But it hadn't done Lucan any good, had it?

"Can we see her?"

Everybody looked at her and Pete. Then some of the anger and shock melted from the air. "Just for a minute," Aunt Steffie said. "She's down at the end of the hall, on the right."

THE SMALL SPACE between the bed and the closed curtain was filled with electronic gadgets. A tall steel rack like a coat stand held a plastic bag, fat with dark liquid that ran down through a plastic tube into Marianne's arm.

Jessie looked at the bag and the tubing, so much like a heart and an artery, and felt deeply sick. It was dead stuff, long dead.

"You're right," Marianne whispered. "But it's better than nothing."

Jessie bent over her. "How come you're awake?"

"I'm getting better." Marianne's white face was crested with red on the cheekbones. They had washed her hair. It spread out like a fiery scarf on the pillow. "Lucan said it would be quick. He said we heal fast."

"We?" Pete echoed, from the other side of the bed.

"Not you." Marianne kept her eyes on Jessie's. "Us. People like us. Like you and me and Lucan. Right, Jessie?"

"She's sick. She's dreaming." Jessie edged toward the gap in the curtain.

Marianne's low laugh sent her out of the room trembling.

She passed doorway after doorway in the long white corridor. Homesickness settled on her like lead. Tendrils of pain clawed at her. Other people's suffering. The smell of dying caught her by the throat. She walked faster, head down. Faster. *Got to get out of here!*

"Don't run in the hallway, please," a nurse said crisply.

126

Chapter 26

Walks Like a Duck

"YOU KNOW WHAT it was like?" Pete said the next morning, as he stood in the darkened kitchen pouring boiling water into Aunt Steffie's biggest teapot. "Like a snake shedding its skin. That's when I finally got it figured out."

"Well, if you've got it figured out, tell me, will you?" Jessie was instantly sorry she'd snapped. Her skull felt like bursting.

"You know it already. You just won't admit it, 'cause it scares you too much."

"Don't make me think, Pete. I feel like death."

She'd wakened early to see Aunt Steffie bending over her, a black shape against the painful morning light. Steffie was going to the hospital to sit with Marianne, and would Jessie be all right by herself?

"Wish I could stay home... both of you in bad shape... that terrible business last night... "

The words came to Jessie in clots. She muttered something, and Steffie covered the windows and went away. Jessie sank into dreams of wandering lost in dark tunnels, while something tiptoed just out of sight behind her.

When it finally leaped out of hiding and began screaming at her, she saw it was only a small green-black lizard, nothing to be scared of. Except it wouldn't stop screaming. *Ow...*

She surfaced slowly. Grey light leaked around the curtains. Jessie buried her head under the blanket but the shrilling started up again.

Not a dream. Not the phone. The doorbell. Someone was leaning on it.

Go away!

It went on and on. She pictured a blunt thumb pressed on the button and a mulish face behind the thumb. She dragged herself out of bed and into a robe and down the stairs. Then hid behind the door, away from the touch of the light, to let him in.

"What are you doing here?" She yawned and rubbed her aching temples. "Why aren't you at school?"

"It's Saturday." Pete looked her over, frowning.

"I'm sick. I'm going back to bed."

"Oh, no, you're not." He grabbed her by the arm and towed her into the kitchen, where the blinds were still closed.

Jessie was too worn out to fight. She sat at the table with her head in her hands while he talked over his shoulder at her about snakes shedding their skins. She didn't pay much attention until a steaming mug clunked down under her nose.

"Drink up."

"I don't want it."

"But you need it. Go on, drink!" He stood there, arms crossed, waiting.

Because it was the only way to turn him off, she curved her hands around the cup. It felt like holding the sun. Comfort seeped into her with the heat. She took a sip. Gasped and nearly dropped the cup. "What is this?"

"Just tea, with lemon juice and honey. My Gran gives it to me when I'm sick."

"Yeah, it does taste like medicine." But she took another sip. The lemon burst against the roof of her mouth like a small bomb. The bitter earthiness of the tea worked its way up her nose. The honey's flowery sweetness made her dizzy.

128

"Helps, right?" Pete took a gulp from his own mug. "I figured it would. You need something in your stomach."

"I guess I do feel a bit more awake. A bit more normal." Whether it was the tea that had done the trick, or just Pete being there, she didn't know.

"Good. Now, what we gotta do is figure out how to fix you."

"Fix me? I'm not broken, I'm just sick!"

"Don't argue. I've been watching you for days, getting more and more like Lucan. At first I thought it was just a sickness, but now we know what he really was, eh?"

She banged her mug down. "And what was that?"

Pete looked at her calmly. "A vampire."

She laughed.

"Yeah, it sounds stupid. But you know what they say. If it walks like a duck, and quacks like a duck, and has feathers like a duck, then it's a duck."

"But, Pete!" Images mobbed her. Lucan's teeth bared at the moon. How he'd deadened Kenny's mind. How he'd slid himself and Marianne out that little window. His dead, cold body. The sudden leap of his pulse at sunset.

And her cut palm, smarting in his bloody grip. The pain of light, the growing pull of darkness. The hunger.

She hid her trembling hands under the table. "Come on, stop clowning. Vampires are just a story that somebody made up!"

Pete was by the stove again with the mugs, pouring more tea. "A lot of it's got to be stories. Turning into bats and flying around. Sleeping in coffins. Things like that. But think about it. What started the stories in the first place?"

He added an extra dollop of honey to Jessie's cup, stirred it and carried both cups to the table.

"They could be a sort of mutation," Jessie said. "I tried to tell

129

Marianne that yesterday. She wouldn't listen." Thinking of Marianne, she shivered.

"They could be. Maybe they mutated so much over the years, they're not really human any more. That's what I thought when I saw Erasmus last night, washing off his old skin. Like a snake. Not human at all."

"Funny." Jessie rubbed her goosebumped arms. "How much he looked like Lucan, after."

"Family likeness."

"Maybe." She gulped down some tea. It tasted less like medicine now. "Just one problem. Marianne and me... Pete, you can't catch a mutation. It's not like a germ. It's something you're born with. What's happening to us?"

"That's what we have to find out. And fix." He scratched his chin. "Only, I can't think of a doctor who'd give us the time of day."

"I wish Dad was here." Clement's face floated into her mind, with its warning eyes. Then, as if the second thought was hooked to the first, she pictured a sky-blue business card with silver printing. "I wonder... "

Pete kicked her ankle gently. "What?"

"Why would my father go to a psychic?"

"Your dad? Go to a psychic?" Pete laughed. "No way!"

She told him what she'd found in her father's wallet.

"Huh. Worth checking out," Pete said. "Get the card and get dressed and let's go. Unless you want me to fry you up some bacon and eggs first."

She clutched her lurching stomach and scraped back her chair. "No, I'll get dressed!"

"And no crawling back into bed." He looked at his watch. "If you're not down in ten minutes I'll go up and haul you out by the ankles."

THEY WALKED PAST the place twice before they found it. It was like any of the other big, shabby old houses that lined King Street after you crossed the bridge to the west side, except that it was perched on a tall stone foundation that went right down into the river.

The second time, they spotted a small black-and-white sign on the brick wall beside the front door:

EUGENIA PALMER

HERBS - DREAM WORK - HOROSCOPES

It was a dusky noon, the sky heavy with purple clouds. Jessie wore dark sunglasses and a yellow rubber rain slicker with a hood that shaded her face, but she felt the invisible sun. It hung over her like a sword. Suppose there was a break in the clouds, a stray beam?

What would happen? Would I turn into a little pile of ashes?

It was a relief when they stepped inside the front door, which wasn't locked, and shut it behind them. They stood in a hallway with closed doors left and right. The doors had brass numbers, 1A and 1B, at chest height, buttons for door bells beside them, and name labels under the buttons. A weak electric glow struggled through the amber panes of a glass box on the ceiling.

This place looked even older than Aunt Steffie's house. The walls were panelled in dark varnished wood up to about shoulder height. Above that was faded wallpaper in a pattern of leaves and flowers.

Jessie took off her sunglasses, pushed back her hood and drew in a deep breath. Then she choked and gagged. Pete frowned at her. "What's the matter?"

"The stink," she said, muffled behind her hand.

He sniffed. "Doesn't smell bad. Kind of sharp and spicy. Must be those herbs."

"I can't breathe. Got to get out." The odour was ferociously bad.

She could feel it creeping over her skin and soaking into her hair. Her stinging eyes sent rivers down her cheeks. Nausea pressed up inside.

She turned and fumbled toward the outer door. Then a latch rattled behind her and she swung around to see a tall, thin shadow step into the corridor. Golden highlights shone on cheeks the colour of strong coffee.

A voice said, "Who... "

Then dead silence.

Jessie was thinking of making another move for the door when the dark woman dashed back into the room she'd come from and two seconds later burst out again, a bunch of feathery leaves in her fist. She thrust them at Jessie's face.

"You! You get out of my house!" The shout rang through Jessie's head. More followed, but by then she was falling, falling into darkness, and all she heard was *night thing... evil... destroy...*

They've found me out, was her last conscious thought. They're going to drive a stake through my heart.

Chapter 27

A Bit of a Tiger

SOMETHING WAS tickling Jessie's nose. She pushed it away with a shaky hand and opened her eyes. It was a frond of Boston fern hanging from a pot above her head. She was lying on her back on a sofa, with rain beating on a window behind her. Her slicker and dark glasses were gone.

"Feeling better?" A dry voice, deep for a woman's.

The room was full of a watery green light. Even filtered through rain and dozens of plants that hung from the ceiling or climbed strings tacked to the window frame, it was still too bright for comfort. Jessie shut her eyes again.

"Jess?" Pete plumped down on the sofa at her feet.

"I'm okay." Still with her eyes closed, she pushed and pulled herself until she was sitting up. She took a deep breath, then coughed. The air was spiky with odours. Among the smells were tiny flickers of animal life. In the darkness behind her eyelids she could see them, bright red sparks darting through the jungle of odours.

Three feet in front of her burned a blue flame the size and shape of a person.

Jessie's eyes snapped open. A woman sat on a chair facing her. An orange cat, its fur on end, glared at her from the woman's lap. A thin, dark hand smoothed the rough fur.

"I won't offer you anything to drink," Eugenia Palmer said coolly, "because, to be honest, I don't want you to stay. It's hard for me to sit here so close to you. After you leave I'll have to cleanse the place, and that won't be a simple matter."

"Fine. If you don't want me here, I'll go." Jessie pulled her legs under her and pushed against the sofa. She sank back.

Eugenia's laugh was deep and rich. "Don't take it personally. Pete's told me enough about this... affliction... that I know you didn't bring it on yourself. I'm not so sure about Marianne. What can I do for you?"

Jessie leaned sideways and tugged the photo of her father and herself out of her back jeans pocket. She handed it over. Eugenia studied it for a moment, then turned her hard, black gaze on Jessie's face.

"I liked Clement Brown. He was a good man. But that doesn't tell me a thing about you."

"He came to you for help. Why didn't you help him?"

"I did. Best thing I could do for him was give him this advice: Stay away from August Erasmus!" She scratched the cat's ears thoughtfully. "He wouldn't listen. Said he had to do something. He felt responsible."

"For what?" Jessie leaned forward. She already knew there was no comfort to be found in Eugenia Palmer. But there might be truth.

"He'd done some work for Erasmus, and he was afraid his work would be used for something cruel. But he couldn't remember what he'd done or seen in that house. Except in dreams. He thought maybe Erasmus had hypnotized him."

"So he came to you..."

"To help him sort out those dreams."

"I don't understand," Pete put in. "Why didn't he go to a doctor?"

"Right, or the pastor at our church," Jessie said. "Why you?"

"I asked him that. Your dad was a very conventional man." Eugenia's white grin flashed and faded. "But he was no fool. He knew

134

he was mixed up in bad business. Bad, dark and deep. Your pastor would have been a little lost lamb in that darkness, and your dad knew it."

Pete stuck out his chin. "And what are you?"

"Just a bit of a tiger," Eugenia said softly, stroking the cat's fur. A spark crackled off the orange back.

Jessie cleared her throat. The smells were becoming a little easier to take. "Did you help him remember?"

"Yes. He got it all back. Wouldn't tell me everything, though: didn't want me involved. He said he knew now what Erasmus was. And he had a responsibility to get rid of him. To destroy him. He asked me how to do it."

"That's it!" Pete bounced up from the couch. "That's what we want to know too."

"I'll tell you what I told him. You won't like the answer any better than he did. It's almost impossible to destroy things like Erasmus."

Pete sat down again. Jessie's eyes followed Eugenia's stroking hand. "*Almost* impossible."

"That's right. Because they're like bindweed. You know bindweed, with the pretty white flowers? If you just cut off the stems, the plant will send out shoots in another place. You have to dig down deep and find the tap root, and pull that."

"You mean," Pete said, "it won't do any good to get rid of Dr. Erasmus?"

"No good at all. He's just one of the stems. Like Marianne. Like Jessie."

Jessie opened her mouth to protest but Eugenia's hand chopped the air. "You asked. Now listen. You need to find the ancestor, the one who got them started on this road. That's the tap root. That's where you've got to cut them off."

"Then we're out of luck." Jessie rubbed her prickling eyes. "I know where the first Erasmus is. Lucan told me. His name is Gabriel and they buried him 400 years ago. In the Netherlands."

"He might as well be on Saturn!" Pete thumped his knee.

"Unless they brought him with them," Eugenia said. "When they emigrated."

Jessie made a face. "Brought a corpse?"

"Hey! She's right!" Pete jumped up again. "If it was that important to them, would they leave it behind, where anybody could get at it?"

"Okay, tell me straight." Jessie looked at Eugenia. "You're saying we have to find the first of the Erasmuses and dig him up. And then what?"

"And do whatever you have to do. Silver, sunlight, and salt would all come in useful. And ash wood for the stake."

"Stake!"

Eugenia threw back her head and laughed. "Your faces! I know, I know. Vampire-slaying is not part of a typical Saturday afternoon here in Finnismore. This is beer and baseball country."

"There must be some other way!" Jessie protested.

"If there is a way, it's just this. To keep fighting. They can't change your nature, they can't force you to be like them. That's a line you have to cross of your own free will."

Jessie sat up straight. "Then if it's just will power... "

"It isn't. It's a disease, and you've got it. Oh, there are some good signs. You can still go out by day, you can breathe in my house. Maybe, because you got infected through an act of kindness, you're not as far along that road as another would be. But you *are* on that road, girl."

Eugenia shooed the cat from her lap, stood up and set her hands on her hips. "One thing you must not do. And that's feed."

136

"I … I don't know what you mean."

"You know exactly what I mean! Take living blood. Do that, and there's no going back. You'll be like them. You'll be lost."

Hunger cramped Jessie's stomach. She swallowed a mouthful of saliva.

"Another thing. Whatever you do, get it done before nightfall." She glanced at the rain-drenched window.

"Because Erasmus will be up and about after that?" Pete said. "Sure. That just makes sense."

"There's more. He'll have allies, you don't know who. But Jessie," she pointed a long forefinger, "when the sun goes down you won't be fighting just them. You'll be fighting yourself. So don't come back here after dark, looking for protection. You'll find my doors and windows sealed with salt."

"Thanks," Jessie said bitterly. She tried pushing herself off the sofa again and this time wobbled to her feet. Pete stepped up behind her and took her arm. Eugenia blocked their way.

"Again, nothing personal. I just wouldn't risk myself around you. And you, Pete, that goes double for you. When night falls, you get yourself indoors. If she knocks, don't answer."

"You mean, run out on Jessie? Are you crazy?"

"Friendship won't protect you if she changes. You get behind locked doors. Better yet, what's your church?"

"I, uh, don't really have one, personally."

Eugenia clicked her tongue and Pete said hastily, "My grandmother goes to Mary Magdalene, over on Erin Street. I go with her sometimes."

"Isn't that the one they're burying August Erasmus from?"

"August? Don't you mean Lucan?" Jessie felt confused.

"They're saying it's August," Pete said. "Gran told me Lucan's paying a lot of money to have a vigil held. You know, prayers and

137

candles around the coffin, day and night until the funeral on Monday. Gran thinks he's such a wonderful son."

Eugenia grinned. "Much good will it do either of them! Never mind, if you're caught out after nightfall, go there."

"But will it be safe?" Jessie wondered. "Being in the church with whoever it is?"

"Oh, that corpse won't rise from its coffin. Unless I'm guessing all wrong." Eugenia turned abruptly, crossed to the back of the room and vanished through a curtain of ferns and ivy. The cat slipped after her. Jessie hadn't even seen a door on that side.

They heard her moving about in the next room, then her alto voice. "I picked up a few hints from Clement, and I remember some things from when I was young. There's never been more than one Erasmus around at a time. They have a funny way of burying one generation just as the next comes into its own."

The ivy rustled and she was back, holding two small clear plastic envelopes. "I recall the old man, Marcus, from forty years back. And I recall when August came to town. He was about the same age Lucan is now. It wasn't many days before Marcus was dead." She held out the packets. "Pete, these are for you."

He took them and sniffed at them. One was full of white crystals that looked like sugar, the other was packed with dry, broken leaves. Jessie backed away. The stink that had felled her at the door came clear through the plastic.

"What *is* that?"

"Aconite." Eugenia was watching her. "Also known as wolf's bane."

Pete's eyes met Jessie's, then slid away. She felt cold all over. Just for a moment, he had been afraid. *Pete afraid of me!*

"I gave some to Jessie's father," Eugenia said. "Don't go using it for tea, by the way. It's poisonous."

138

"Yikes." Pete shoved the envelope into his pocket. "What's this other one? Cyanide?"

"Salt."

"Just salt?"

"There's no 'just' about it. Salt has special power against evil. It corrodes, and too much of it can kill, but it also heals and cleanses. Don't take it for granted just because you like it on your chips."

Pete still looked doubtful, but he slipped the packet into the pocket of his windbreaker with the other one.

"Wolf's bane didn't save my parents," Jessie said. She led the way out into the front hall, on legs that at last felt strong enough to hold her weight. Her slicker hung on a coat stand in the corner, the dark glasses in the pocket. She put them on.

With her hand on the door knob, she stopped. "And suppose we do find the first Erasmus, and we dig him up and destroy him."

"Well?" Eugenia cradled the orange cat in her arms.

"If we do that, what about Marianne? Could it hurt her?"

"It could. It might kill her. Along with the other stems."

"Kill her?" Pete echoed.

Jessie let go of the knob. "But then we can't do it!"

"Or it could set her free. Depends how deep she's gone, and for how long. Either way, alive or dead, she'd be free. But, Jessie …" For the first and only time, Eugenia reached out and touched Jessie's arm with the tip of a finger. "The same goes for you. It's going to be kill or cure."

Chapter 28

Graveyard Search

JESSIE SCRAPED a little more dirt from the stone with a stick. "M." Inch by inch, the letters came clear. "U. And here's an S."

She sat back on her heels and rubbed her forehead with the back of a grimy hand. "Pete!"

"Found something?" He dropped to a crouch beside her.

"Maybe. This one ends in MUS."

"With our luck, it'll be Remus or, or Titmus. Is that a name?"

Using a piece of cedar shingle he'd found, he dug away more of the layer of fibrous dirt that covered the name on the gravestone. First SMUS. Then ASMUS. Then...

"Erasmus!" Jessie dropped her stick, squeezed in beside him and scrabbled at the dirt with her blackened fingernails.

"Born Rotterdam." Pete slapped the stone triumphantly. "See that? In ... uh ... 1798." He frowned. "That can't be right."

"Died Finnismore, Canada, 1856." She scrubbed the name clean with her palm. "It's Willem Erasmus. It's not the right one!" She groaned. "I should have known it couldn't be that easy."

"Look at that." Pete pointed. Above the name, where you'd expect to find a cherub's head or a cross, was a carved row of moon shapes, the four phases. "At least we know we're in the right neighbourhood."

"But even if Gabriel's buried around here, we'll never find him before dark."

Jessie crawled away from the stone and crouched in the shadow of the dripping cedar hedge, turning her back to the brightening west and pulling the hood of her slicker across her face. For the past hour the cloud layer had been getting thinner. The sun kept reaching out to stab at her.

She buried her face against her knees. So cold, so sick, so tired. *I just want to crawl into the dark and die.*

"Jess? You okay?" Pete touched her shoulder.

She lifted her head and forced a smile. "Just great."

After leaving Eugenia Palmer's house, they had gone to Finnismore town hall, where the local archives was, and struggled with card indexes and heavy volumes. When they came out again into the rain, all they knew was that there was no record of where the Erasmuses had buried their dead before 1900.

"And we've wasted a good hour and a half," Pete said.

"They've got to be somewhere! I wonder how many cemeteries there are in Finnismore?"

It took them another hour to find out. Only about half of the town's population was walking around above ground. The other half was underneath.

Most of them were in the municipal cemetery, on the west edge of town. But every old church had its cluster of grave markers at the side or back. And more, they discovered by asking, were built into the foundations of old houses and old stone walls.

When Pete spotted the pioneer graveyard, screened from the newer part of the town cemetery by a cedar hedge, he laughed. "Jess! Pay dirt!"

"And if we find him? Then what?"

They never did decide what they'd do if they found a stone in-scribed Gabriel Erasmus.

Willem's stone was the twelfth they uncovered in the oldest part of the pioneer cemetery, where the slabs lay flat and the grass had grown high. Year after year, soil and moss and leaf mould had collected around the edges of the stones, then more and more, working inward. Now many of the stones were covered, and grass had grown up over them. You had to look for the grave-sized dips in the turf, then scrape down through grass and earth to find the cold touch of stone.

One good thing, as Pete pointed out: you could still read the names on most of the buried stones. Their earthen coverings had protected them. The ones that had stood in the rain, wind and snow were scoured nearly blank.

Pete ran his hand over one that stood near: a smooth marble slab with a few dints in its face. "Look at that! It might be the one we're looking for, and we'd never know."

"You'd think I'd know. If what Eugenia said was true. If Gabriel is the root and I'm a stem." She touched the standing slab and shook her head. "Remember when Dr. Erasmus came to my house, looking for Lucan?"

"Yeah. You didn't want me to open the door."

"I knew he was there before he rang the bell. And another time, I touched Lucan. From a distance."

"Touched?"

"He was sleeping." She shivered. "No, he was dead. It was horrible."

"So you could find the old guy if he's around here?"

"Maybe. Gotta try."

They crawled out from under the cedars. Jessie stood up, brushed wet leaves off her knees and settled the dark glasses on her nose. She turned her back on the west.

A parting shot from the sun reddened the grass and stones. Two shadows leaped to the far edge of the field.

"Getting late," Pete said. "Better hurry."

"Time for you to go home. Eugenia said."

"Not without you."

She held out a hand and he took it and squeezed, and let go. Then she braced her feet and closed her eyes.

Right beside her stood a blazing light. Pete, so solid, so calm, radiated hope and worry and determination like a halogen bulb. She couldn't see anything in the darkness around him.

Try! Little by little, she blocked him out. Then came the small signs all around. No thoughts, just fluttering, slinking, quivering bits of life.

Farther. Deeper.

Jessie trembled. Blood. Blood everywhere. A web of red life bubbled across the countryside, knotting here, breaking off there. Calling to her.

Not that! Deeper. But what was she looking for? Anything strange, out of place, wrong.

Dead.

Dead air. Pure black. Stone. Cold, dry, silent. Old. *Old.* Years on years on years.

Where? Reach. Stretch. Where?

Here, it answered. Suddenly, dead then alive. Far. Deadly. Like lightning behind dark hills. *Here!*

"No!"

"Jess?"

She pushed back her hood. Her body told her the sun was gone. A glance over her shoulder showed a rusty red sky shading upward into purple. She took off her sunglasses and put them in her pocket.

"Well?" Pete demanded.

"There's something out there." She pointed east. "What it is, I don't know. But it doesn't feel like Lucan or August. It feels older, and... and not so human." *And now it knows about me, it knows I'm looking.*

"Then let's go and find it." Pete picked his way between the graves toward the gate. "Hurry! It's getting late."

"It's already too late." She put down her head and passed him, walking fast. Her feet itched to run. He was trotting when he caught up to her on the road.

"We can't wait for another day," he said.

"That's my problem, not yours. You heard what Eugenia said. You've got to go home!"

"I'm not afraid of you, Jessie."

"Lie," she said softly. But strangely enough, his lie made her feel less desperate.

They walked east along the muddy road. The first houses lay two cornfields distant, eyes of yellow light just starting to open.

Pete laughed uneasily. "This really is the dead end of town. Nobody around but us!"

No cars passed them. Nobody else was walking or biking on the road, so far as they could see.

Jessie wasn't sure when she began to feel somebody behind them. The first time she felt the chill, she glanced back. The road stretched away empty.

"What?" Pete looked back, then searched her face.

"Nothing, probably." They faced east again and Jessie walked faster. The shadows deepened in the ruts. The red light faded from the sky.

The second time, it was like a cold hand touching her between the shoulder blades. She stopped and turned around. Searched the road and the fields on both sides. Nothing.

"Come on," she said. "Hurry!"

They walked on into the dusk. The lights of town bobbed nearer. Then the road dipped between two high banks crested with tall pines, and night dropped on them like a sack.

Something's there.

Jessie took one more glance over her shoulder and stopped dead. Lucan, walking three strides behind them, met her eyes and smiled.

Chapter 29

Gabriel

"DON'T YOU KNOW me, Jessie? Pete?" He spread his arms wide. "It's me! Lucan!"

"It is and it isn't," Pete muttered. Jessie nodded. The boy looked like Lucan, exactly. The same sort of dark pants and sweater, with a dark nylon jacket like Pete's over top. The jacket was just for looks on this chilly night, she knew, so that people wouldn't wonder. He wouldn't need it.

The same thin, clever features. The same ice-blue eyes, silver now in the dark. The same long, pale, silken hair that floated in every breath of air. The same. And yet... No.

"You're not Lucan," Jessie said. "You're not even a boy." There, that was it. Those eyes knew too much, they'd lived too long.

Pete's fists knotted and he moved closer to Jessie. "We saw you kill him. We know who you are. You're August."

"Sure, are you?" That secretive smile again. He sauntered across the road, hands in his hip pockets, and perched on a boulder that jutted from the grassy bank below a pine tree. "Just so you know: what you saw last night was not a murder."

Jessie watched him carefully. He looked relaxed, his back against the pine trunk, but he was waiting for something. "What would you call it?"

"A blending. Lucan is in here." He placed a long hand on his chest. "And here." He touched his forehead. "We're all in here."

"We?" Pete echoed. "All?"

146

"All."

For a moment Jessie stared, baffled. Then she pulled in a quick breath. "I get it." She backed off a step. "You're the first. You're Gabriel!"

"Not even that. Not precisely." His eyes went cloudy and inward-looking. "I was Gabriel, once. There was a time... I was old. Rotting inside. Wealth, rank, name, they did me no good. I remember being afraid... afraid of dying... "

He made a sudden gesture with one hand, tossing something aside. Then smiled his closed-mouth smile again, his eyes bright and focused. "But I found a way out of that. It's been several centuries, Jessie, since I've been afraid of anything at all. I have become much, much more than Gabriel."

"By sucking the life out of all your children," she flashed. "By stealing their bodies!"

"Wrong!" He spread his arms. "This body belongs to us all, renewed with each generation, with each baptism of blood and moonlight. And none of us is dead. We all share our life. All of our memories are alive. Don't you think that's wonderful?"

"I think that's disgusting," Pete said.

Gabriel ignored him and kept his eyes on Jessie's.

"Pete's right," she said. "Did you ask Lucan if he wanted to be blended? Did you give him a choice?"

"He didn't understand, then. Any more than you do." He stood up, stretched like a cat, slipped his hands back in his pockets. "Now he understands. And he's happy."

"I don't believe it!"

"Then find out for yourself. Ask him."

"Ask?" She searched his face. "How?"

"You know how. I'm open. To you. To nobody else. Go ahead, Jessie." He planted his feet and lifted his chin, bracing himself. "This should prove how much I trust you."

"All right, I will." She focused on his eyes.

"What's this?" Pete hissed. "What are you doing?"

His hand was on her arm but the touch was miles away. She was somewhere else. Groping through fog. *Lucan?* She reached out, found nothing. Stretched farther, deeper. Then, yes, there it was, just a whiff of him, but thick with terror.

And from far away a desolate voice. *Jessie, help me!*
Lucan!

His answer faded as she reached for it, leaving her alone in the fog. With blackness closing in like jaws on every side.

She poured herself outward. The jaws snapped just outside her skin. She stood in the road, flattened against Pete. Gabriel's grin was wide and sharp and gleaming white. "You're quick," he said. "I like that."

The pines rustled at the top of the bank. A slim figure slid down to the road and stood on the other side of Pete and Jessie, between them and the lights of town.

"Marianne? Is that you?" Pete peered at her. "What are you doing here? Why aren't you in the hospital?"

"I'm better." She had a new, husky voice. Somewhere she had found a stained T-shirt and torn pants, and a pair of dirty sneakers with broken laces. The old Marianne wouldn't have been caught dead in an outfit like that. *Now she has been,* Jessie thought, and would have laughed except she knew if she did, she'd melt into hysteria.

"We've got to take her back." Pete took a step. Jessie caught his arm before he could take another.

"We're trapped! Don't you see?"

Marianne shook back her tangled mane and drifted toward them. On the other side, Gabriel sauntered closer.

"Don't be afraid, Jessie," he said. "You're safe. I don't relish

148

blood from my own kind."

"I'm not your kind!"

He laughed. "You are. Believe me, I know."

"What do you want?" She and Pete were back to back now. She held him tight by the wrist. She didn't trust him not to try and rescue Marianne. And if Marianne got her hands on him...

Gabriel stood two paces away, just beyond arm's reach. "Acknowledge my position as leader. I can't tolerate rivals. Become my vassal, like Marianne, and all will be well."

"Vassal! Slave, you mean. You think I'd ever say yes to that?" Then something struck home. "What about Pete?"

He made a what-can-you-do gesture with both hands. "Pete is not our kind," he said simply.

"I'm hungry," whispered Marianne.

Pete's wrist tensed under Jessie's fingers. Now he understood. She felt his other hand move, sliding into his jacket pocket.

If it were just me, Jessie thought, I'd have a chance. The deepening night sent energy sizzling through her body. Fear would give her the edge she needed.

But Pete could never outrun them, never match them for strength. His safety lay with the lights of houses, a field's width away.

Gabriel took another step. He lifted a hand toward Pete.

A crackle of plastic came to Jessie's sharpened ears. Then a taint in her nostrils. *All right, Pete!*

"Now!" he yelled.

Marianne leaped. Jessie clapped her hand to her mouth and nose as Pete's hand swept from his pocket. The air was full of salt and leaf fragments: blinding, sickening. Jessie felt Marianne bounce off her, heard a retching sound. Then she and Pete were pounding along the road toward the lights of town.

"We'll make it!" Jessie gasped. But next instant the beat of their feet had a quicker echo. Pete was flying, but not fast enough.

She didn't have to look back. Gabriel ran three strides behind them: she felt him there, knew the precise distance. Two strides. An arm's length.

Then out of a lane to the right shot two dazzling white beams of light. They swung, sliced the air and flared into Jessie's eyes.

She shrieked and waved wildly with one arm while shielding her eyes with the other. The car squealed to a halt beside her. Still half blind, she felt her way along the fender and pawed at the window. It slid down.

"What d'you think you were doing, running in the middle of the road? You could have been killed!" A woman's voice, furious.

"It's dark, and we thought someone was following us. Thanks for stopping! Could you give us a lift? Please!"

"Us?" The woman pulled her head back. "Aren't you alone?"

"No, there's me and him." She turned to wave at Pete, but he wasn't there. Nobody was there.

"I only saw one person, you. Is there somebody else hiding around here?" The window slid up. Gravel flew and the car's tail-lights vanished around a bend. Jessie stood alone in the middle of the empty road.

"Pete?" She shook with sudden fear. "Pete!"

Someone laughed at her out of the dark, but it wasn't Pete.

Chapter 30

Pete Lost

"MRS. OLIVEIRI? Is Pete in?"

Pete's grandmother held the door two inches open and stared through the gap with eyes like black stones. Jessie kept smiling, but it was hard. She wanted to lean back, to push the air away from her face. The sour smell of old age hung in the doorway.

"No. He's not in."

Of course he wouldn't be here. They wouldn't let him go that easily. He might be lying under a drift of leaves, wrung out like a dishcloth. Or he might be walking the streets, looking for her. Changed, like Marianne.

After an hour of prowling the back alleys, calling, probing the dark places under verandas and in culverts, this was the last place she'd thought of looking. His home.

"Did he phone?"

"He did not phone. Who are you to ask?"

"I'm Jessie! Jessie Brown. Pete's friend."

"Oh no, you're not!"

"But you know me! I've been here!"

"You're not Jessie." The gap narrowed. A reek of fear and hate flooded out, driving Jessie backward. "I don't know what you are, but you're not her. Stay away from Peter!"

The door slammed.

Jessie backed away to the street. In the lit windows on the second storey of Oliveiri's Pet Emporium, where the family lived above the shop, a curtain jerked closed, then another, and another.

Horrible, wasn't she? said a voice in her head.

It wasn't her own thought. The voice was strange and at the same time familiar. There was a laugh in it. *Think: how wonderful never to be like that. Never to get old.*

"Everybody gets old." She headed down the street, darting glances up lanes and under hedges. Find Gabriel's burial place. But first, find Pete.

Not everybody gets old. Not our kind. Don't you want to stay young forever?

"If it means being like you, killing my own children, then no."

You don't mean that. Think about it! To stink, with your flesh dying on your bones. To grow so feeble you can't even walk on your own. To sit drooling, to forget everything. And at the end, for what? Just to rot away into dust.

An old man and woman walked past, slow and careful, each gripping the other's veined hand, each with a cane in the other hand. The smell of old age surrounded them. Horror flooded Jessie's mind and she ran. Nowhere: anywhere, just to get away from the smell of that dying flesh.

A block away, in the parking lot next to the high school, she stopped and threw her head back to suck in streams of moonlight. She unzipped her rain slicker and let the cool night air blow the odour of age from her mind and body.

Easy to see what was going on. "He's messing me around!" She kicked at the asphalt. "He's playing games with my head."

But why? When he first came after her and Pete, what had they been doing? She thought back. They had left the pioneer cemetery and were heading east, looking for something. What? Whatever she'd sensed when she reached out for Gabriel. His grave?

Bad time to look. Sunset. He'd wakened and felt her touch and come after her, with Marianne at his heels.

East. That's where I felt it. Suppose she reached for it now? Could she find the place, with Gabriel out of it? *If I can find it, I just have to last this night. Then tomorrow, we'll go and...*

"Jessie!"

She spun around and searched across the parking lot. "Pete?"

"Jessie, help me!"

A shadow moved on the other side of the chain-link fence that divided the parking lot from the sports field. Jessie pulled off her slicker, dropped it on the asphalt and started running. "Pete, wait!"

She was over the fence in seconds, but by then the shadow had vanished up the lane toward McClure Street. It moved in a strangely jerky way, as if somebody much stronger, but invisible in the darkness, was hauling it along by the collar.

As she reached McClure Street, the shadow passed under a streetlight and Pete's dark head appeared. He was alone, but he still moved in that clumsy, unnatural way. And, funny thing! No matter how fast she ran, he stayed ahead.

It was midnight. The moon was still nearly full, the sky clear as a glass lens. The strong white light sucked the orange from the glow of the street lights. Pete's hair reflected a cold greenish glint as he ran.

A police cruiser prowled past the end of the street. Jessie leaped back behind a hedge. It passed within two feet of Pete, but the officer didn't slow down, didn't even turn his head.

"Pete! Stop!"

He glanced back, then stumbled on. Around a corner onto Mercy Street and west, toward King Street and the bridge over the river. By the time Jessie reached the corner, the jerky figure was a block ahead of her. The steel girders of the bridge jutted above him.

He slowed for a moment, but only to climb onto the railing of the bridge. He stood up, he teetered. And then, as Jessie skidded onto the bridge and threw herself at the railing, he leaped.

One moment spread out like a starfish in the moonlight, then gone.

Jessie gripped the railing and stared down into the swirling black water. Finnismore's river was hardly big enough to notice, most seasons. But the last few days of rain had swollen it. Now it was big enough to drown in.

"Pete!"

"Not to worry," said a lazy voice to her left. Gabriel leaned his elbows on the railing and smiled down at the river.

Pete's head broke the surface near the far shore. A moment later he crawled out onto the grassy bank. And then he kept crawling. The moonlight glistened on his shiny back. He slithered under a bush and out of sight.

"That's not Pete! That's one of your pukey hounds!"

Gabriel laughed. "They aren't pukey at all. They're marvellous hybrids, the product of two hundred years of bioengineering. All my own work, too."

"I don't care what they are! Where's Pete? What have you done to him?"

"Not a thing. He's walking free right now. Listen!"

There it was again, Pete's voice, calling her name. It came to her strangely from below, muffled, and she realized he must be under the bridge. On this side of the river. Here, a path ran along the water's edge, with a strip of grassy land and small trees and flower beds next to it on the landward side.

Pete's voice grew louder. Looking over the railing, Jessie saw the top of his head move out from under the bridge. He was walking fast, searching from left to right, but there wasn't anything unnatural now about the way he moved. It really was him.

"Jessie! Where are you?"

154

Here! I'm up here! But the words never left her mouth. She couldn't make her lips move. Gabriel leaned on the railing and smirked at her.

Pete! He wasn't alone down there. A slim, dark shape melded against a tree trunk, so still he didn't see it as he passed. But Jessie saw it separate from the tree and drift along the path behind him. He didn't look back.

"She could take him any time now," Gabriel said mildly.

"Why are you doing this?" Jessie backed away from him. "Where's the real Pete?"

"He's down there. Really and truly! I'd move fast, if I were you."

He was right. She knew, as she turned and dashed to the end of the bridge, that Gabriel was yanking her around on a string. But still she had no choice.

She leaped down the stone stairs that led to the strip of parkland, raced along the path beside the river. And there they were, far ahead: Pete still calling, still searching from side to side. And a pace behind him, the soundless shadow.

Suddenly he stopped and whirled around, and even from here Jessie could see his face whiten.

He stood like stone, while the shadow drifted closer. A slim hand reached up to his throat. He didn't move.

Jessie saved her breath and sprinted.

Chapter 31

Hunger

THE LAST FEW yards were a blur. The expression on Marianne's face, though, when she swung her around by the arm... Jessie didn't think she'd ever forget that. Marianne shrieked her frustration at the sky. Then she tensed to attack.

"Stop it!" Jessie grabbed her by both arms and shook her 'til her hair thrashed. "You're not an animal! You're Marianne! You're human!"

Marianne sank back, but she glowered. "I want," she muttered in her husky new voice. "I'm hungry."

"No use talking to her," Gabriel said over Jessie's shoulder. "At this stage, so soon after changing, she only understands the language of blood. Really a very simple and primitive creature. But of course she's no threat to you. Only to ordinary people."

Jessie turned and backed away, still holding Marianne by the arms like a shield. "Make her leave Pete alone."

"You make her. You can do it, you know. She's under your control right now."

"My control?" Jessie pulled her hands away. Marianne stood looking at her from under her matted hair like a cornered wolf. She didn't move.

"Pete," Jessie muttered, afraid to raise her voice in case it broke whatever spell held Marianne. "Get out of here."

He gave a sudden jump, as if he'd just wakened out of a dream. He looked around, his eyes skidding past her. Then he jogged away along the path, calling her name.

Gabriel stood on a flat rock at the water's edge and stirred the surface with the toe of his shoe. "I give Marianne to you," he said casually. "Here's your chance to do some real good, Jessie. Tell her to jump in the river and drown, and she'll do it."

"What? No!"

"What else can you do? If you let her go, she'll find Pete again. Or someone else. Her mom and dad, for certain. Then they'll be just like her." He stepped away from the water. "Come on, Jessie. Think of all the innocent lives you'll save. Use your power!"

What he said made sense. There was no other choice. But, but! Thoughts mobbed her head. One leaped out at her. "It would be wrong."

"Wrong?" His pale eyes opened wide. "To destroy a monster? Wrong to protect the innocent?"

"She was innocent too. Used to be. If I did that to her I'd be just like you." There, that was another thing she needed to remember. "It would be the same as taking blood."

"High-minded but stupid. You've lost your chance. Marianne!"

"Yesss... "

"Go."

Her eyes lit up. She whirled and ran.

"Marianne! Stop!" Marianne didn't stop. "Call her back!"

Gabriel laughed and walked away toward the bridge.

Jessie raced after Marianne.

SHE NEVER FOUND Marianne, never found Pete. Hours later, or at least it felt like hours, she folded down to the sidewalk at the base of a hydro pole. She didn't even know where she was. The houses looked unfamiliar.

Tears ran down her cheeks. Pete. Marianne. They were gone,

they were lost, and she was trapped in a nightmare, and when the sun rose it would kill her.

A police cruiser drifted along the street toward her. Somebody was sitting in the front seat next to the cop, somebody she knew. Wasn't that Aunt Steffie? Why would she be out in a police car? Oh, of course. *Looking for me. Looking for Marianne. Well, they've found me.*

But the police car drifted past, rounded the corner and cruised away.

Gabriel's laughter floated down to her. "They can't see you, Jessie. You're starting to fade. And no wonder! Don't you know you're starving to death?"

She looked up. Gabriel stood twelve feet above her head, one foot on a steel piton driven into the wooden hydro pole. He held the other out to the side, toe pointed, like a ballet dancer. His hands were in his pockets.

He laughed again and leaped into space, and then he was gone too, and she was alone on the sidewalk.

A sudden ferocious emptiness gnawed at her gut. She fought it down and pushed it back into the deep place where she'd had it locked up, afraid of it without being fully aware of it.

She was aware of it now, though, clawing up from the deep place. *How long can I keep that down?*

The moon had dropped from midnight. Only a few hours of darkness left. *I just have to last that long, and then...*

And then what? Another day like today? No, it would be worse.

And what about Pete? What about Marianne?

She rubbed her forehead. What *was I doing before I saw Pete? Something important. Something that could help us. Looking. For what?*

She tried to focus, tried to remember. Her brains were scrambled like spaghetti.

East. That was all that came to mind.

Jessie climbed to her feet, faced east and closed her eyes. East. Yes, something was there. A cold, dark place with the weight of years on it. Empty, but only hours ago filled with death.

Not where I want to go. But I have to find it.

She walked away from the hydro pole, following her nose. It was easy at first. The death trail was clear as a stream of smoke in still air. And once she got moving, she sped along with the ease of wind in the grass. She felt as if her flesh and bones were made of light.

Night poured through her, all its scents and sounds.

Words out of houses, clear through brick and wood and aluminum. Arguments, laughter, love words, hate words. Red radiant anger. And all around, everywhere: bird life, insect life, globules of pure energy.

Tiny mouthfuls. *No. I didn't think that.*

Jessie stopped under a huge silver maple, a grandfather tree. The life-pricked shadows called to her. A hand to the trunk: sap cooling inside, sinking toward winter. The bark still warm with stored sunlight. The skin of her palm soaked it up.

There's something I should be doing. What is it? With so much life buzzing and sparking around her, she couldn't keep her mind straight.

A big white moth brushed past her face and she caught it and held it cupped in her hands. A rag of moonlight, quivering with life.

Jessie wondered: *Could it keep me going? Would it be the same as taking... what Eugenia said?*

A giggle trickled down to her from up in the tree. "Not much in it. Hardly worth the effort."

"Marianne?" Jessie looked up. Two glowing eyes narrowed at her from the branches above.

"You're way, way far gone." Marianne giggled again. "You're starving! You can't even think!"

Jessie opened her hands and watched the moth flutter off into the darkness. East, it flew. East. The death trail. She drifted on down the street past big houses where fear and anger and love slept behind dark windows.

Halfway along the street stood a bus shelter. A hut with Plexiglas sides, each panel a dark mirror. Her reflection came to meet her as she walked toward it. From behind her another police car shot past, impaling her body with its headlights. Her face and hands were gauzy and glowing in the dark mirror, like sheer curtains lit from inside.

"You're fading away," Marianne whispered from behind the bus shelter. Gabriel laughed somewhere in the distance.

Jessie reached the baseball diamond and then knew she wasn't going to get any farther. She fell on her knees on the outfield turf, lay down flat, and rolled over to let the moonlight wash her face.

That helped, but it wasn't enough. *I'd need to swallow the whole moon.*

A crackle in her back pocket reminded her of comfort. She turned on her side, tugged the photo out and held it close to her eyes. Her father's face spoke to her. *Stick it out, Jessie. Don't forget. Don't give up!*

"Don't give up what?" Then she remembered. East. "Why do I keep forgetting? What's wrong with me?"

Strength flowed into her from Clement's face. Enough strength to help her struggle to her feet.

And then the photo flared in her hand. She screamed as the yellow fire seared her fingers. A charred scrap fell to the turf.

"You don't need that," Gabriel said. He stood on the pitcher's mound, feet apart, hands in pockets. Marianne crouched behind him and glowered from under his elbow. Yards back, close to home plate,

160

the grey man stood watching, his hands humbly folded.

Jessie hardly saw any of them because between her and them stood Pete, his head bent, face in shadow. He'd lost his windbreaker, and his shirt, too. His arms and chest were bare.

Gabriel took a hand from his pocket and waved at Pete. "This is what you need, Jessie. Go on, Pete."

Pete walked slowly toward Jessie. His arms were white in the moonlight.

"Pete? Are you all right?"

He said nothing.

"Aren't you cold like that? Pete?"

He took a pen-knife from his jeans pocket and opened it. Then he held out his left arm and placed the blade against the soft skin between the wrist and the elbow, on the inside.

"Pete, no! No!"

"You have to feed or you'll die." It was his voice but all wrong, flat and dead. "I don't want you to die."

"Pete, stop! Look at me!"

His eyes looked through her into nowhere. Then the knife bit and the blood welled out. Life trickled down his arm, dark and rich and shining. Jessie backed away. Or thought she had. But suddenly she was nearer.

Her hunger clawed its way out. It took control of her body and moved her legs and lifted her hands.

"Feed," he said in the same dead voice. "Or die."

She watched Gabriel watching her, soundlessly laughing. So clever, so cruel. He could have chosen any poor soul to destroy her. But he'd chosen Pete.

The part of her that was still Jessie watched in horror as her hands reached out, closed their fingers around Pete's left wrist and pulled his arm to her mouth.

Chapter 32
Child of Darkness

JESSIE THOUGHT later that this was something Gabriel should have known. He should have guessed that touching Pete, touching his blood, could have more than one effect on her.

It wasn't like lifting a cup. It was like opening a door. All of Pete's fear and horror spilled down his arm and into her mind. All his memories, all his hopes. And, at bottom, the rock of courage that was himself.

Oh, Pete.

"Take it!" Gabriel said. "Take it and live."

"Drink," Marianne whispered, creeping closer. "Drink!"

Jessie's grip slid in the blood running down Pete's arm. It felt like hot silk. It smelled like copper and lightning.

Pictures trickled into her mind. Pete cradling a hurt gerbil in his hands. Pete sitting shoulder to shoulder with her in a narrow staircase, monsters above and monsters below. Pete thumping a cup of hot, sweet tea on the table in front of her. "You need it. Go on, drink!"

"Well? Go on," Gabriel said. "Drink!"

Jessie let out the breath she'd been holding. "I won't."

"You will," he answered reasonably. "You have no choice. If you don't, you'll starve to death."

"Didn't you tell me to use my power?"

He grinned, not bothering now to hide the long, sharp canine teeth. "What power?"

162

No point arguing. He wouldn't know what she meant. For the first time it came to her that Gabriel had weaknesses. Until this minute she'd thought that with his centuries of hoarded wisdom and cultivated power, he must know everything. That he could do anything. That he could read her like a book.

But he didn't know everything. He only understood his own kind of power. If she was a book, she was one that was closed to him.

Jessie slid her hand down Pete's wrist and clasped his hand. His fingers tightened around hers. Strength flowed into her from the touch. Strength freely given. Enough to let her shove hunger back into its pit and lock it up.

Pete's eyes looked dazed, but alive. He was himself.

"Come on," she said. Hand in hand, they walked across the outfield toward Jasper Street. Energy came back to Jessie's bones and muscles with every step.

When they reached the street, she felt Pete flinch. Gabriel was waiting for them under a streetlight.

"Don't waste your time, Jessie. You haven't got much left."

They walked past. She didn't look at him.

"He's following," Pete muttered.

"He's curious. He doesn't understand why I'm still holding out."

THE CHURCH of St. Mary Magdalene loomed like a castle over the street of shabby bungalows. Above the western door, the rose window glowed softly in the night.

"Weird to think of August Erasmus's body lying in there," she said. "No: Lucan's body, really. With people saying prayers around it."

"It's just a body," Pete said. "Nothing good or bad about it. Don't let it bother you." He was sitting on the bottom step, scrubbing blood off his arm with a wadded tissue and some of his own spit. Jessie

163

tried not to watch.

"That'll do for now." He dropped the tissue into the bushes beside the steps, stood up and started up the stairs. Then stopped and looked back. "Come on! I'm freezing here without my shirt!"

"You go in. I can't."

"Why not?" He tipped his head sideways at the church. "Maybe the priest can help. Maybe he'll give us something we can use, something blessed. You can't fight those guys all by yourself, and without any weapons."

The rose window pulsed at Jessie. There was power there, all right, but it didn't pull at her. It pushed. She was afraid to let it touch her. Still, being afraid was no longer an excuse for anything, was it?

"I suppose it couldn't hurt to try." She followed him up the stairs. As she climbed she tried to relax, to open up to what lay above her.

Needles of light stabbed from a hairline crack around the arched door.

"Pete, wait! I, I don't think... "

He was hauling at the heavy door. It swung open suddenly. Golden light slammed Jessie to her knees. Not just the light. The incense, whiff of hot wax, the voices chanting... *et spiritu sancti...*

The door thudded shut and Pete was crouching beside her, halfway down the steps. Her head cleared a little. Enough to let her pull herself together and clench her senses shut again.

"Latin prayers and incense!" She laughed unsteadily. "He's getting the works!"

"You can't go in." Pete sat back, horrified. As if he'd only just realized what that said about her.

"I can't go in." She looked up at the rose window. Shut out. Lost. Child of darkness. She would have wept if she'd had any tears, but they were all dried up.

"All right, I'll go in and get help."

164

"Get help?" She grabbed his shoulder to help pull herself to her feet. "Eugenia was right. There is no help." She gave him a push. "Go on in!"

"But where will you go?"

"I don't know." She set her teeth. It was getting harder and harder to keep a brave face on. "This night has been forever!" Then a stray thought. "I saw police cars out and about, and Aunt Steffie too, but they never saw me. I wonder if they're looking for me? They must know Marianne's gone missing. They'd be looking for her, for sure."

"Yeah, and my parents'll chew me out five ways from Sunday when they get hold of me." Pete sounded almost cheerful. "The priest is sure to phone them, when he sees me like this." He held out his bare arms, then let them drop. He turned and climbed the last couple of steps, then stopped and looked at the sky. "Won't be long 'til the night's over. What then?"

She looked. The moon was sinking. Dawn was coming. What then? She tried not to imagine the worst. "One way or another, this'll be over."

"Where will you be when the sun comes up?"

"I haven't a clue. Don't worry, I'll find somewhere."

"I'll come and find you."

"Pete, you'll never get away from your family again, not in a million years!"

"They won't be able to stop me." The light from the crack around the door rayed across his face, mulish as ever. Then he pulled it open and stepped inside, and the door closed.

"There, he's safe now," she said aloud. *Safe from them, and safe from me. And I'm totally alone.*

A voice laughed at her out of the night. *Oh, no, Jessie. You're never alone. Not while you have me.*

165

Chapter 33

World of Wonders

JESSIE STOOD on top of a stone wall under a tree and gazed across the lawn at the Erasmus mansion. The house was dark except for the smaller top storey, which caught the last of the moonlight and glowed like a jar full of fireflies.

The death trail had led her here at last. Death soaked the whole grounds, now that she was attuned to it. The gardens, the house, the grass, the trees, they all reeked of it. Old, old death.

But where now? I can't dig up the whole place, she thought. Even if I had time.

"Jessie, why fight it?"

She whipped around. He was walking toward her along the wall, arms outstretched to the sides as if he needed them for balance. "You can't win, you know. I've made thousands like Marianne. And they've made thousands. Someday it will be millions." He veered his arms like airplane wings. "A glorious army of Mariannes!"

"And then I suppose they'll rule the world."

"Very likely. You can't stop it, so why not join it? Why not give in gracefully?"

"Why should I quit now?"

"You're running on moonlight and adrenaline." He stopped next to the tree trunk. "We're different from ordinary people, Jessie. We're only half flesh. The other half is pure energy. But you've almost worn out both parts. You're going to snuff out like a candle."

"Like you care."

"Well, I don't, really." Idly, he traced the fissures in the tree trunk with his fingers. "It was pleasant, though, for a few days, to have a friend. Remember that first moonlight run, hand in hand? I'll treasure that memory for a long, long time."

"You stole it from Lucan." Jessie jumped from the wall. She thudded lightly down onto the lawn.

"Jessie! Come with me again!"

Startled, she gazed up at him. With the sinking moon behind him, making a halo of his floating hair, he really could have been Lucan: secretive, strange, frighteningly strong. Lonely, young. Full of wild life.

"Come with me again!" he called. "You can't imagine what's out there. You don't know what powers lie sleeping inside you."

"I don't want to know."

"I don't believe that! Remember that time on the bleachers, you almost thought you could fly?" Before she could answer he threw himself into the air. For impossibly long moments he soared above her head, skimming the shadows under the tree's topmost boughs.

Then he dropped to earth and vanished. She gasped.

"Over here!"

She spun around. Out of nowhere he landed like a leaf on the grass.

"How did you work that?" Then she nodded. "I get it! Shadows. You used the shadows, didn't you?"

"Did I?"

"That has to be it! You can shape darkness the same way you shape light. Right? To create illusions. That's how you fooled me into chasing Pete: the fake Pete."

He shrugged, smiling. "Maybe. Maybe not. You have a lot to learn. But, Jessie, you're got infinite time for learning. Why not use it?" He whirled in a circle, arms wide. "Endless life, endless possibilities. You could be anything at all! Master any art, any science. Like me."

She shook her head and turned away. It was too hard to think when he was talking at her. *Think! There was something I had to do.*

"Jessie, don't you get it? You're being offered the whole world."

He was in front of her again, beaming at her. A sense of vast space opened around her. *The whole world.*

"All you have to do," he said softly, "is stop being so stubborn. Just give in."

Take care, Jessie. Take care.

Her head buzzed. So many voices!

Anything I want. But there was a catch, wasn't there? She pressed her hands over her eyes, shutting him out, shutting out the moonlight. *Oh, of course! What's the matter with my head?* Her hands dropped. "I could be anything I want, right? Except human."

"Oh, Jessie, Jessie." Gabriel shook his head at her, all smiling patience. "Why would you want to be human? You and I, we're top of the food chain. Humans are *dinner*."

Her head cleared. Suddenly it was as plain as daylight. "You see, that's the whole problem right there." She looked past him at the eastern sky, where the trees made a ragged black border along the horizon. The sky above them was violet.

I had something to do, something important, she thought. There's a reason why I came here. She made a wide circle around Gabriel and headed toward the house.

He was suddenly in front of her again, dancing backwards, laughing. Jessie stopped at the moondial. "You've been messing me around all night. Playing games. What for?"

He tilted his head thoughtfully. "I suspect it's Lucan's influence. The boy had a playful streak, and I find I'm enjoying myself more than I've done in several generations. It's a bonus, since all I expected to gain was his vitality."

"You just soaked him up."

He walked around the moondial to the other side and leaned on it, bracing his forearms. "Naturally, the lesser feeds the greater. With each renewal, each added life, I grow and I learn. The Erasmus name is highly respected. Who knows what I might become, given a few more lives? How could you possibly *not* want to be like me?"

"How come you're still lurking around Finnismore? Isn't this town awfully small for a wonder like you?"

"Of course it is! I outgrew Finnismore long ago. If you'll recall, August was often away. Soon, I, or Lucan, will be off to college, and after that the world will be his oyster. But Finnismore will always be home." His eyes shone with laughter. "He'll always come back. You might say his heart is here."

"You don't have a heart. It's something else that's here." *Something I have to find.*

"Really? What could that possibly be?"

"I don't know."

He shrugged and touched the brass gnomon that stuck up like a tooth from the moondial's face. Jessie knew he was still playing with her, but she had no clue how.

"All I know is, you don't want me to find it. Everything that happened tonight was just to keep me from following my nose, wasn't it?" It was coming to her now, coming clearer and clearer. "All this talk, too. It's to keep me from finding out where this... this heart... is buried."

He stared at her coldly. Beyond his head, there were no stars in the sky.

"I don't understand why you didn't just kill me."

"I almost did." His shoulder flicked. "Several times. It would have been much easier than trying to make you see reason."

169

"Then why?"

"Something always stopped me. I think it was Lucan." He smiled, as if remembering a favourite child. "He really did want to avoid hurting you. I think you were the first person who ever tried to be his friend. That seemed to leave a deep impression on him." The smile died. "But he's gone now, Jessie."

She thought of Lucan's distant, despairing cry inside the darkness that was Gabriel. She took a step back.

"Time's up," he said. "It's late. For Lucan's sake, I'll take you to shelter now." He held out a hand.

"Shelter? With you?"

"Not what you're thinking." The points of his teeth showed. "No coffins. No boxes filled with earth from the old country. There are light-proof rooms under the house. Clean beds, all amenities. Come with me now."

"No. I won't crawl into the dark with you."

He laughed. "It's your funeral, then." He watched her as she backed away, but he made no move to go anywhere himself. He stood gripping the moondial's edge.

A row of figures flashed in her head. Four figures: the phases of the moon, cut in stone. On a tombstone. Willem Erasmus.

No, somewhere else. Another stone. Jessie shut her eyes tight and scrabbled for the memory. Different shape, different place.

And then she saw, and wondered why she hadn't seen it long before this. It was as if someone had set a stopper in her mind, a block so subtle she hadn't even known it was there.

She opened her eyes. While she'd been working the thought through a maze in her brain, he had slipped past the moondial and was flowing at her across the grass.

Jessie dashed the last of his control from her brain and turned and ran, ran as never before. In seconds she was at the wall, she'd

170

swarmed up and over. Almost over. A hand clamped on her ankle and she was caught, sprawled half over the wall.

"No time," he hissed. "No time for you either, Jessie. You won't last five minutes past daybreak. You'll roast!"

The grip on her ankle was suddenly gone. She sat up on the wall and looked back across the lawn. It was empty.

The eastern sky blushed pink. Jessie was perched on top of a wall under a cloudless sky, her head and arms bare. Through a mesh of thinning trees, a scarlet sliver slid up over the edge of the world.

Chapter 34

Salt and Sunlight

JESSIE LAY FLATTENED against the base of the wall, cool stones at her back and a pitifully thin screen of lilac bushes in front. Clear through the wall she felt the sun, a giant steel hammer pounding at her spine.

Oh, Pete, where are you?

Darkness pressed up from the damp earth. It crept up around her, wrapped her around, tried to drag her down into sleep. She fought it off by watching the shadow of the wall as its edge inched down the trees across the street.

Hours yet until that shadow passes me. But when it does, good-bye Jessie. She touched the raw, blistered left side of her face. All that took was one soft kiss of morning sunlight.

Pete, hurry! Hurry!

Feet thudded past her on the road. Pete, clutching an armload of something, making for the iron gate.

"Pete!" she whispered.

The feet skidded on the pavement. The lilacs thrashed. He knelt beside her, crushing the branches. He dumped his backpack at her feet. "Your face!"

"Touch of sunburn." She tried to laugh. "How did you know I was here?"

"Hunch. Figured you'd be around here somewhere. East, that was where we had to look, didn't you say so? Where else but the Erasmus place? Here, sit up."

"You found your jacket. And your shirt." That seemed to her miraculous.

"My dad found them by the river last night. He thought... " His mouth tightened. "Never mind. Can you sit up?"

She sat up and he slid a pair of dark glasses over her eyes. Then pulled something woolly over her head and face and over the glasses. She could still see, but the threat of the sky was not so fierce. On the burned side of her face, the wool scraped like wire.

"This is a loan from Eugenia Palmer. Glasses, ski mask, coat." He held the thick, dark wool duffle coat so she could slide her arms into the sleeves. "Pull up the hood over the ski mask. And now the gloves."

"All this is hers? We owe her."

"You bet. Specially for answering her door at the crack of dawn. I did have to do some pounding. Now, you stay under cover 'til I can find the damn thing."

"Wait. I know where it is. Did she lend you a spade, too?"

"I got one out of our garden shed. The salt's from our cupboard." He pulled a cylinder-shaped cardboard box out of his pack. "Tell me where it is."

"I have to be there with you." She struggled to her feet.

"Jess, you can't! The sun!"

"I *have* to be there."

He opened his mouth to argue, then shut it. "Come on, then. Which way?"

She told him. He picked up the spade in one hand, cradled the box of salt in the crook of that arm, and slipped the other arm around her.

She pushed his arm away. "Thanks, I can walk by myself." One step, and her knees gave way.

"Come on," he said patiently. He hauled her to her feet again and

173

together they staggered along the wall to the gate.

"Pete. Without you I'd be dead."

"Forget it."

"Dead or worse."

"We're not out of the woods yet."

The gate stood open an inch. They stepped into the sunlight that flooded through the bars. Jessie fought the urge to fall flat, to press herself into the earth.

Light hammered her through the veil of fabric. It drilled at her bones. Against her closed eyelids and the dark lenses it was a raging fire.

Pete swung the gate open. They started across the lawn. The ground lurched under her feet. Too many steps to count. Then suddenly she was on her face in the cool grass, with darkness feathering across her closed eyes. She risked a glance through slitted eyelids.

Brilliant green stems and leaves, each rimmed in scarlet fire, stirred across the painful light. She was lying with her head in the patch of asters, beside the pedestal of the moondial. With a shaky hand she traced the moon phases cut into the stone.

"Goodbye," she said. "Goodbye for good."

She pushed at the pedestal. It didn't budge. Pete knelt beside her and wedged his shoulder against the pedestal, under the disc of the dial. He heaved. It rocked, but didn't fall. He heaved again and it toppled over, crushing the asters.

Where the base had been was an octagon of bare earth about eighteen inches across. Cold air breathed from it. A tendril of mist curled up to touch Jessie's cheek.

"Down there." Pete scowled at the bare patch, layering disgust over top of fear. "Okay. Here we go."

He picked up the spade and set furiously to work. Chunks of earth and clumps of turf flew. The hole grew wider and deeper, and breathed colder. Then, too soon, the spade rang on stone. The sound set Jessie's teeth on edge.

Pete dropped the spade. "I've hit a rock! We're in the wrong place!"

"It's not a rock."

He glanced at her, wet his lips, grabbed the spade and dug up more earth. Then he used the blade to scrape clean the surface of what he'd found. Jessie crawled forward and leaned over the hole.

A stone. Flat grey granite, with four shapes cut into its length. No name.

"A tombstone? Down here?" Pete asked.

"The moondial was the tombstone. This is the coffin."

"Coffin. Okay." Pete took a deep breath and set to work again. Once the earth was cleared from the whole stone, they saw it was more than six feet long and two feet wide. "It's a coffin, all right," Pete said. Grime smeared his cheeks. "A stone coffin. But it's only buried two feet deep!"

"That was enough."

Jessie was fighting the darkness again. It reached up to her from the hole, cold dark air that wrapped her up and pulled her down. All she had to do was close her eyes and sink down, out of the cruel sun, down into the cool, kind earth. How sweet, how easy.

"All right!" Pete slapped a hand on his leg. "Let's get it open. No use waiting around." Terror leaped from his skin. Jessie marvelled at him. Anybody else that scared would have been miles away by now. Not Pete.

He wedged the point of the spade under the edge of the stone slab, and pushed. Nothing moved. He strained, strained...

The slab lifted, quivered, grated over the stone edge beneath, and fell back with a damp thud against the side of the hole. Pete dropped the spade and jumped away.

Jessie hauled herself forward on her elbows. She looked.

Sunlight touched brown bones. Gold glinted on the spiky hand. Blackened rags of what might have been velvet clung to the ribcage. Shrivelled scraps of leather wrapped the feet.

"It's not … not so terrible," she tried to say. But her heart was trying to climb into her throat. The skull was tilted up, the fanged jaws frozen in a tiger's snarl.

"Bones," Pete said loudly. "Nothing but dirty old bones."

"The sun's on them," Jessie said. "Something should happen. It's going wrong!"

"Eugenia said to use salt." Pete grabbed the box from the grass where he'd dropped it and pried at the round lid.

A shriek pulled Jessie's head around. Across the lawn came a wild-haired figure, crawling. Suddenly it pitched forward and lay with its hair over its face.

"Marianne!" Pete started toward her, then looked back at Jessie and the open grave. He cursed and ran back, tore off the lid of the box and held it out at arm's length. Salt poured down onto the bones.

In the same instant, from deep in the earth, from everywhere and nowhere at once, came a howl of agony. The ground trembled.

It seemed to last forever. And then the cry died from the air. But inside Jessie, in her veins and arteries and brain and in the marrow of her bones, the scream went on and on.

Pete was still pouring salt. It fell in a glittering stream. More and more slowly it fell, until Jessie could count each drifting crystal.

The bones gleamed, as if the sun had grown stronger. The gleam sharpened to a dazzle. Then they smoked. Last came a hot blue flame that shot straight up.

The same fire burned Jessie's body. Fire scoured every vein. Every cell was burning. She looked down at her hands and saw blue flames hissing from her fingertips.

176

She wanted to scream but could make no sound. Above her, Pete moved like someone in a slow-motion film, intent on what he was doing, not looking at her.

Sound died around her. The asters bent silently under the breeze. Their scarlet haloes faded, their green went dusty.

Everything's going away. Everything's dying.

Even the pain was numbed.

The blue flames still speared up from the coffin, veiling the ancient bones. The toppled moondial, lying at the edge of the grave, cracked in the heat. The pedestal broke into pieces. A flake of stone flew up lazily and nicked Jessie's arm. A moment later blood welled sluggishly from the cut. She felt nothing.

It's killing me. She couldn't even feel afraid.

Chapter 35

The Grey Man

SOMEONE CAME walking across the lawn. The grey man, the servant. Jessie felt no surprise. Pete went on strewing salt with wide, slow sweeps of his arm. He didn't seem to see the man, and Jessie couldn't move or speak to warn him.

The grey man's unremarkable clothing and colourless hair didn't stir in the breeze. Beyond him everything looked dim. Under his feet the grass was darkened. As if a cloud of *nothing* travelled with him: a nothing that sucked up the sunlight and colour and life from everything it touched.

He stopped on the other side of the open grave and looked across the flames at Jessie. The fire burned lower.

Pete shook out the last of the salt and dropped the box. It hit the grass and slowly bounced. He turned and glided toward Marianne.

"You've lost it all," said the grey man, though his mouth never moved. His voice was a dusty whisper.

"Lost?"

"The extra senses. Power over other minds. Flesh made half of light. Life everlasting. All gone."

"We've done something right, anyway. We've got rid of your precious Gabriel."

"So you have." He glanced down at the coffin.

The flames had died, leaving the stone box coated with a layer of fine ash. Already the wind was licking at it, picking it up and puffing it away.

"He was a useful tool. He sent many to my kingdom. But a fool, in the end," the grey man said. "He gave you the power to find him, and so he was destroyed. And thousands of his making with him." There was no regret or pity in his voice. There was nothing in his voice at all.

Then he looked at Jessie and smiled the smile that came from a million miles away, the smile she'd seen through a broken car window.

"You owe me a debt."

Ice touched her heart. "Who are you?"

"You're strong. I can use that strength. A suitable replacement for my servant Gabriel."

"Never! I'll never serve you!"

"You will. Some day, when memory has betrayed you, when the things that happened in these few days no longer seem real."

"How could I ever forget what happened to me, or Marianne, or Pete? Or Lucan?"

Suddenly she could move. Looking over her shoulder, she saw Pete kneeling by Marianne, cradling her head in his arms. Marianne lay limp, her eyes closed.

When Jessie looked back across the grave, the grey man was gone. But a voice still whispered dustily in her mind.

You will be like everyone else. Years will pass, and you will grow old and tired. Life will corrupt you. Truth and lies will blur until you don't know the difference. Good and evil will become shades of the same grey. It may take half a lifetime, but it will happen. I will wait.

She listened, every hair on end.

You will belong to me.

Then the breeze blew clean.

It struck her then that she could feel it, a cool tickle through the wool mesh of the ski mask. I'm not dead, anyway, she thought, and

179

recklessly tore off the mask and threw the dark glasses onto the grass. She peeled the gloves from her hands and shrugged off the coat.

The sunlight made her squint, but its touch on her skin was like a hug. She held up her face and spread her arms to feel it all over.

"Forget life everlasting." She laughed. "This is enough!"

She got up and staggered to where Pete still cradled Marianne. "How is she?"

"Her face and hands are burned, but not too bad. Don't know where she was holed up, but she couldn't have been out in the sun that long." He looked up. "You good?"

"I'm wonderful!"

"Yeah." He looked her over and nodded. "Yeah."

Marianne's eyes fluttered open. She gaped up at the faces hovering above her, winced, lifted a hand to touch her cheek, then abruptly sat up.

"Where is this? How did I get here? What happened?" She looked down at herself. "Why am I wearing these awful clothes?"

"It's a long story." Pete looked at Jessie. "What are we going to tell her parents?" He closed his eyes briefly. "What are we going to tell mine?"

Jessie thought about it. "We'll say Marianne went a bit nuts and ran away from the hospital."

"Nuts?" Marianne's eyes widened. "Hospital?"

"And we went looking for her."

"Okay, good." Pete nodded. "That'll take the edge off when they get hold of me."

"And it's the truth, sort of."

Truth and lies will blur.

"Just a sec," Jessie said. Stronger now, able to walk without lurching, she went back to the grave. The wind had scoured out the coating of ash. There was nothing there now but an empty stone box.

180

Quickly, using the spade, she shoved most of the earth back into the hole. Then she searched in the wreck of the moondial until she found what she wanted.

Pete was helping Marianne to her feet by the time Jessie came back with Eugenia Palmer's coat over her arm, the gloves, ski mask and sunglasses stuffed in the pockets. She held out what she'd found.

"What's that?" he asked.

It was a flake of stone the size of her palm. A circle was cut into it. "A full moon. It's from the moondial."

"What, a souvenir?" He shook his head. "Why would you want to remember any of this? Better try to forget."

"Oh, no." Jessie took Marianne's other arm and they started across the lawn toward the gate. "I don't ever want to forget."

You will belong to me.

"Never," Jessie said.

About the author

PATRICIA BOW lives in Kitchener, Ontario. She has written several other books for young people. To find out more about Patricia and her work, visit www.execulink.com/~thebows/patricia.htm.

www.ingramcontent.com/pod-product-compliance
Lightning Source LLC
Chambersburg PA
CBHW072139170626
46813CB00004BA/1620